Toby Smith and The Fifth Element

by
Jeff Dale

Bloomington, IN

authorHOUSE®

Milton Keynes, UK

AuthorHouse™
1663 Liberty Drive, Suite 200
Bloomington, IN 47403
www.authorhouse.com
Phone: 1-800-839-8640

AuthorHouse™ UK Ltd.
500 Avebury Boulevard
Central Milton Keynes, MK9 2BE
www.authorhouse.co.uk
Phone: 08001974150

First published by AuthorHouse 8/31/2006

ISBN: 1-4259-5487-1 (sc)

Printed in the United States of America
Bloomington, Indiana

This book is printed on acid-free paper.

To Doris & Nathan

Special thanks to Alison, Gary & Angela, Ian, Malcolm & Cath, Andy & Jo.

Chapter One
The Broken Clock

Toby sat on the edge of his bed rubbing his aching eyes. Suddenly realising that it was Monday, he moaned miserably "ughh, school." Knowing that his Mother would be calling him again soon, he stretched and tottered off wearily across the landing. Before he reached the sanctuary of the bathroom though, she shouted up the stairs "come on or you'll be late."

Freezing in his tracks, he called back feebly. "Sorry Mum, I'll be down in a minute." Stumbling blindly into the bathroom he slipped out of his warm pyjamas and crawled into the shower. "At least it's not P-E today" he sighed as he enjoyed the refreshing hot water. Having stayed up nearly all night repairing a broken toaster, that had been shooting pieces of burnt toast into orbit, he knew that only a good night's sleep would really ease his tiredness. Promising himself that this had to be the last time that he stayed up late he decided to go to bed earlier that night. Especially as his Mum, who was already suspicious, had said that it just wasn't natural for him to be tired all the time. She had also suggested that he should see the Doctor for a check up. Putting all that on the back burner for now, he continued enjoying the torrent of stimulating hot water until she yelled up from the bottom of the stairs as expected "I won't call you again." Raising her voice to another level she added impatiently, "oh and if you're not down here in the next five minutes you're grounded!"

Realising by her tone that this was definitely his final warning, he got out of the shower immediately. Grabbing a clean towel off the rail, he noticed his reflection in the large mirror. Wiping away a patch of steam, he studied his long thin face and sticky out ears. He moved closer, staring dejectedly at the tiny image that was looking forlornly back at him with its pasty white face and overly large green eyes, topped off with its ridiculous mop of curly red hair. Sighing, he thought that it really wasn't that surprising that his nicknames at school were the "carrot top kid" and the "human match," with the latter usually reserved for gym when he wore his old white tee-shirt and shorts. Although he knew that he could cope with the constant teasing about his appearance, he had to admit that he really did hate his hair colour for it was that which he felt really made him stand out from the other kids. As he wondered what the coming day would bring. He heard his Mother's insistent shout that he should hurry up again, turning his back on the tiny sparrow like image, he ran back into his bedroom and put on his school uniform. Hoping that his Mother wasn't too angry about him getting up late yet again. As he sat at the kitchen table eating his cereal she eyed him suspiciously as she buttered hot toast, "do you feel all right" she asked him? Looking concerned.

"Why?" he answered quietly wondering what was on her mind.

"You look tired" she said "sleeping okay?"

Nearly choking upon his mouthful of bran, he answered sheepishly "yeah I'm fine."

Not convinced by his mumbled reply she leaned on the table "are you sure?" she asked.

Toby knew that he couldn't let her find out that he'd been awake virtually all night. Deciding reluctantly that his only option was to lie, he stuttered "I, I think that there's a bug going around the school and I'm probably coming down with it."

Not going to be fobbed off that easily she declared "well if that's the case, I'll ring the surgery and get you a Doctor's appointment."

Toby grimaced realising that he'd made a serious mistake. Trying to calm her fears, he said quickly "no need for that, if I get an early night I'll be fine by tomorrow."

Walking around the table, she put her hand upon his forehead saying "well I must admit that you don't feel that hot but I think that we'd better let the Doctor examine you anyway, just to make sure."

Toby searched for a way out but not being able to think of one, he came to the conclusion that the only sensible answer was to run. Grabbing a piece of toast he headed for the front door. Unfortunately as he grabbed his school bag from the coat hook in the hallway he turned to find his Mum blocking his path “well are you going to tell me what’s really going on?” she demanded.

Caught like a rat in a trap, he tried a different approach. “Look Mum if you really must know I’m just feeling a little bit down at the moment.”

Putting her arm around him to comfort him she asked “what’s wrong?”

Taking the opportunity that had unexpectantly presented itself he decided to tell his parent about the problems that he was having at school. “It’s like this” he began slowly, “Roland in my class is always taking the mickey about my red hair, and at my age I should be wearing long trousers like everybody else!”

Mrs Smith stared into her son’s tearful eyes whispering quietly “why didn’t you say something sooner?”

Toby nestled deeper into his Mother’s arms, and getting a little upset he blurted out unintentionally “how could I burden you with my troubles? Especially since Dad lost his job at the factory.”

Mrs Smith, feeling rather hurt, told him honestly “we may not have as much as some. Like that bloody Roland’s Father for example. But we manage on what your Dad earns from odd jobs.” She hesitated momentarily, searching for the right words. "Yes, I admit that it was a real blow when your Father hurt his back and was unable to keep his other job. But that's how life is sometimes and you just gotta make the most of it."

Toby suddenly felt very selfish about complaining. Kissing his Mother upon the cheek gently he said "sorry Mum, forget I said anything."

Becoming indignant, his Mother responded adamantly. "I won't forget about it at all. The first chance that I get I'll speak to your Dad about getting you some long trousers because we should have done that a long time ago. Then I'll ring up the school and get that Jenkins boy sorted out." Gaining control of her temper, she added softly "but as for your hair love, I can't see what's wrong with it?"

Toby walked over and stared at his reflection in the hallway mirror "he laughs about it being ginger" he complained bitterly.

"That's only his opinion" she argued. "It's what you think about yourself that really matters."

Toby considered her words carefully, and thought that she was probably right. Because he knew that his hair wouldn't really be an issue if Roland didn't keep on about it all the time. So feeling just a little bit better about himself, he fell back into her arms whispering gratefully "thanks Mum, you're the best."

"No problem" she responded, "that's what I'm here for. Now scoot before you are late for school."

Toby opened the door to leave, but hesitated.

"What now?" she asked.

Shutting the door, Toby sat upon the bottom stair. "About Roland" he said.

"What about him" his Mother demanded "what else has he been up to?"

"Nothing" Toby answered. "It's just that I feel a bit sorry for him."

"Why?"

"Well I know that he's a pain in the butt sometimes, but he's got no Mother and his Dad barely speaks to him."

"That's no excuse for being a bully" Mrs Smith cried. "Anyway his Dad's so rich he probably gets everything that he wants."

"Yeah he does, I know that's true" Toby responded. "I've heard kids at school saying it. But you said yourself that money isn't everything. Would you trade Dad for a million quid?"

"No, I wouldn't" she answered. " But this isn't about money it's about how he's making you miserable by calling you silly names."

Toby sat trying to work out what was for the best, deciding that it would be better to leave it for now. He said "don't ring the school yet Mum. Let's wait and see how he is in school today."

"Okay" his Mother agreed reluctantly. "But if he starts on you again, you make sure you tell me."

"I will" Toby promised as he glanced up at the grandfather clock noticing that it was eight thirty. "Crikey Mum I'd better get going" he yelled.

Running as fast as he could, he headed off down Sniffle lane leaving their small two bed roomed cottage behind. Stopping near the corner, he stared back to see his Mother peeking out of the tiny rose covered window. He saw her smile as she blew him a big kiss. "See you later" he shouted as he turned and ran until he reached the park. Where he stopped and took several deep breaths. Sprinting again, until he reached Mount Park School along with several other stragglers, who were also in danger of being late. Running up the long tarmac drive flanked by two rows of large elm trees, he headed towards the main entrance of the modern red brick building. As he passed a sheltered area, where refuse bins were kept a large hand grasped his shoulder roughly from behind. "Where are you going to squirt?" a gruff voice asked.

Recognising the voice without turning around. Toby cringed in fear, realising that it was Roland. "Sorry I got to dash or I'll be late" he muttered meekly, trying to run off.

Squeezing harder the bully whispered "not so fast freak I ain't finished with you yet."

"I'll be late" Toby pleaded desperately, trying to wriggle free again.

Ignoring his plea for mercy the bully ripped open his backpack, threw his sandwiches on the floor and squashed them into a mushy pulp.

Toby watched in disbelief as he crammed his crisps greedily into his mouth. Although he was the most spiteful kid in school, he had never behaved this badly before. Suddenly realising that he'd be hungry all day he shouted "stop or I'll tell!"

Throwing the empty crisps packet down Roland grabbed his defenceless victim by the throat and bellowed angrily “what did you say?” As he sent bits of half chewed crisps flying everywhere.

“I said I’ll, I’ll tell my t,t, teacher” Toby stammered weakly in reply.

Roland pulled him closer and stared directly into his eyes. “Do you know what happens to squealers?” he asked coldly.

Before Toby could answer, Roland put his fingers around his neck.

Realising that something was wrong. Toby became even more afraid and yelled “stop it you’re hurting me.” Looking into his classmate’s glassy eyes. He saw no sign of life, just a dull red light. “Stop it” he yelled again.

Ignoring him, Roland continued squeezing.

Finding it hard to breathe Toby gripped the bigger boy’s arms. Trying to make him loosen his grip, but he was just too strong. “Stop it!” he screamed hoarsely as everything started fading.

A deep voice demanding “stop that” Roland turned around to see a stranger who was putting a big black bicycle into the bike shed. Grinning impertinently he asked gruffly

“who the hell are you?”

He rocked back on his heels as the man responded instantly “I’m Mr Raven the new history teacher so I’ll ask the questions.” Striding over purposefully he stood with his arms on his hips, demanding “what’s going on?”

Determined not to back down Roland answered sarcastically "nothing Sir." This was the usual response he gave when he was caught doing something wrong.

Unconvinced by his plea of innocence, the tall bearded man looked down at Toby's splattered lunch, asking "are you sure?"

"I certainly am Sir" Roland replied confidently.

Bending down the stranger eyed him face to face saying "if you are lying boy I'll have your guts for garters."

Roland hesitated momentarily, and then responded with a smirk. "But I'm not like that Sir."

Ignoring his obvious impertinence the man turned away from him and focused his attention on Toby who was still shaking and struggling to catch his breath. "What have you got to say for yourself?" he asked politely.

Toby, who was still feeling the effects of the viscous and unprovoked attack, was just about to say that he was being picked on. When he glanced sideways at Roland, who was making threatening gestures behind the teacher's back. Gathering his thoughts quickly he croaked hoarsely "nothing Sir."

Not believing him, Mr Raven asked Toby again "are you sure?"

Toby knew that if he complained every time a teacher wasn't around he would become a target. So in what was very intimidating circumstances, he stared up into the concerned man's face stuttering timidly "th, thank you for all your help Sir, but as I said everything's fine."

"Certain?" Mr Raven asked Toby as he watched Roland carefully.

"Yes Sir" Toby whispered."

"We can leave it there for now" Mr Raven said. "But I expect I'll be seeing you again." He warned Roland as he walked away.

As the teacher disappeared around the corner Roland grabbed Toby again. "Now we've got some unfinished business" he growled.

Returning, Mr Raven shouted angrily "I told you to let him go!"

To Toby's surprise, for once, Roland did exactly as he was told.

Within minutes both boys found themselves sat outside the Headmistress's office with Mr Raven watching them like a hawk. When he was subsequently summoned into her office, they were left alone together. "It's your word against mine shrimp" Roland whispered through clenched teeth. "Keep quiet or I'll have you."

Frightened by the bigger boy, Toby just kept looking forward and never answered the threat. Suddenly Roland jumped up and slapped Toby hard, almost knocking him off his chair. "Ow!" He screamed as he rubbed his reddening face with his hand. "Behave, you're in enough trouble already" he yelled.

Leaning right over him Roland whispered quietly in answer. "I ain't got the time for this nonsense right now, so I'll see you later." Then he walked away, whistling.

When Mr Raven returned, he enquired where Roland was. However he did not seem surprised that he'd left. "A bad egg that boy" he remarked soberly, as he hurried off to look for him.

Minutes later Toby was shown into the Headmistress's office by her secretary Mrs Drillman. As the office door shut behind him with a click, he suddenly felt very alone.

Unlike Roland, who was a frequent visitor, this was the first time that he had ever been to see the new school principle Miss Rowena Blakelock, who eyed him with great interest. "We meet at last" she said as she peered at him over the top of her huge black spectacles.

Toby trembled beneath her piercing gaze.

Not taking her eyes off him, she told him quietly. "We've never actually met before have we? But I know such a lot about you."

"Y, you do?" Toby stammered nervously as he felt himself shrinking before her overpowering presence.

"Oh yes" she said "I have been watching you for some time now. I know for example that your Father lost his job at the mill because he injured himself. A proud man you're Father, too proud to take a hand out, that's for sure." Picking up a pencil she twirled it rhythmically in her strong fingers, until it snapped! "You look just like him don't you, but for your Mother's green eyes and red hair." Hardly pausing for breath she added "It was lovely how they met at Brighton beach wasn't it?"

Toby was dumbstruck, and wondered how she knew so much about his parents.

Seeing a look of bewilderment upon his face Mrs Blakelock turned the screw just a little bit more. "I assume you know that your Mother was drowning in the sea until a brave young man swam out and rescued her."

"My Dad?" Toby asked.

"Your Dad" she replied with an air of authority. "Good old Albert Stanley Smith. The rest is history of course. How they became pen pals for several years before eloping to get married. Then after living in that tiny little cottage of theirs for nearly nine years, you came along. Toby Winston Smith, the apple of their eye."

"Gosh!" He exclaimed "I never knew that my Mum nearly drowned when she was young."

"I said that I knew a lot about you didn't I. But that's enough talk for now. Let's have a nice glass of lemonade together shall we?"

"I'm n, not very thirsty Miss" Toby stammered as he spotted a strange looking jug of bubbling green lemonade upon her desk.

"Nonsense" she said as she poured him out a large tumbler. "Surely you can manage a sip or two, just to please me."

"Not really Miss" Toby quickly added "because of me dodgy waterworks."

"There's nothing about that in your medical records?"

Thinking quickly Toby said in answer “that’s because I asked Mum not to tell anyone about it because I get embarrassed.”

“I see” she said as she scrutinised him again over the top of her horn rimmed glasses.

The thought suddenly struck Toby that with her cold grey eyes and long pointed nose. Miss Blakelock looked like a huge predatory bird that was watching a small defenceless frog. Unfortunately for him, he was the frog that was about to be swallowed, still alive and wriggling. He tried to look away, but couldn’t. He was trapped like a rabbit suddenly caught in a car’s headlights. As he was just about to cry Mr Raven returned, breaking the nearly hypnotic spell. “I couldn’t find Roland Jenkins anywhere” he stated as he shut the door.

Miss Blakelock glared at him, responding angrily. “Never mind him; he’ll turn up soon enough.” Regaining her composure quickly, she once again studied the frightened little frog that sat before her. “So are you being bullied” she asked sympathetically?

“N, no miss” Toby stammered meekly. Remembering the threat about what happened to squealers.

Reading his mind, the big bird countered quickly. “There’s no need to be frightened.”

Toby considered telling the truth, but declined the offer thinking that cowardice was probably the better part of valour. Puffing out his chest he stated adamantly. “No thank you Miss, I’ve got nothing more to say.”

Encouraging him again, she asked “but it’s not very likely that Jenkins will be coming back. So you can tell me what has really been going on.” Leaning back on her chair, she stretched out her long spindly body adding. “You see we have been watching him for some time. If you speak out against him now I will make sure that he’s expelled permanently.” She drummed her fingers impatiently upon the polished oak desk, awaiting his answer. Realising that the little frog wasn’t going to be forthcoming. She sighed, saying “very well as you will not co-operate, you can go for now. We can always have another chat later.” Standing up, she walked over to the window and looking out, she asked him casually “by the way, has anything unusual happened to you lately?”

“No Miss” Toby answering instantly.

He felt his stomach tighten. As she turned to face him and demanded in an intimidating manner “are you certain?”

“Y, yes, yes I’m sure” he exclaimed nervously.

“Positive?” she asked him.

“Yes Miss I’m sure” he blustered.

“Very well, Mr Raven will escort you back to your class. Oh and take your lemonade with you, because you may get thirsty later.” As Toby stood to leave, she blew his mind away by whispering softly “see you soon little frog.”

Leaving the glass of fizzy pop upon her desk he followed Mr Raven back to his classroom, as her chilling words kept repeating over and over in his mind. There was just no way that her using that phrase could have been coincidental. The chance of that was simply astronomical. Reaching class, he became even more puzzled about the days strange events. While he sat at his desk, trying to work out just what was going on, Mr Raven was explaining to his form tutor why he was so late, and just for a fleeting moment he thought that he saw red light in his eyes. Then it was gone, and he wondered if he'd really seen it at all or whether it was just his imagination playing tricks on him. As the teacher left the room leaving him to ponder upon all the unanswered questions that were playing on his mind he wondered why Roland had behaved like a raving psychopath. Why there had been a strange red glow in his eyes, the same as in Mr Raven's? And why had the headmistress had acted so strangely? At least I'm free of them for now he thought, although he had the feeling that he'd see her again soon, as well as Roland who would turn up like a bad penny. It was just going to be a matter of being when and where. However with the rest of the day being fairly interesting, he forgot about all the unusual occurrences until home time arrived. Reaching the school gates, he looked both ways twice before running off towards the park, because he knew that Roland would want revenge.

Arriving home safely, he grabbed a drink and handful of biscuits and made for his bedroom.

Coming in from the kitchen, his Mother shouted from the sitting room "hello love, have a good day?"

Keeping quiet about all the odd things that had taken place at school. He answered

"yeah" as he pulled up his shirt collar to conceal the purple bruises on his neck.

"How was that horrible Jenkins boy today?" she added as an afterthought before he could get away.

Feeling guilty about lying to her for the second time, he called back down "he wasn't in school today." As he quickly ducked into his room and shut the door. Feeling safe at last, he ate the biscuits greedily and swilled them down with his orange juice. Spotting an old clock on his bed he looked at it more closely. Looking inside the back he saw that it appeared to be in good condition, apart from being very dirty. Taking the large brass key, he wound it up, but was disappointed when it never started ticking. "Darn it" he muttered "it's broken." Discarding three rusty spare cogs that were tied together with an old piece of twine. He began slowly taking the clock to pieces.

Until his Dad looked in, saying cheerfully "tea in ten minutes."

"Okay" Toby answered, still feeling ravenous. "Where did this old clock come from?" he added curiously.

"An old chap who couldn't pay for some roof repairs talked me into taking it as payment for some work I did. Now as you know, I don't normally take anything other than cash or cheque. But I felt a bit sorry for the old guy." He laughed, adding "he reckons it's worth a few bob though. So if you can repair it, I'll get it valued."

As they ate dinner Mr Smith told them some more about the old man that lived all alone with his large collection of valuable antique clocks. "If it hadn't been for them" he joked "I don't think that he would have bothered having the roof repaired at all. When they all struck on the hour, the noise was so loud that I nearly fell off the roof!"

Toby's Mother sighed as she sipped her tea. "I think that it's disgusting that he lives all alone like that. It's just not right and I blame the government for allowing it to happen. Why can't they give him a nice flat somewhere?"

Toby looked over at his Dad, who was quietly laughing behind his hand as his wife continued criticising the government. When he started pulling comical faces as well, Toby couldn't help giggling.

Catching on, she glared at them both using the face that she normally reserved for travelling salesmen and canvassing politicians. Unable to keep a straight face for very long, she began chuckling too.

When the laughter and evening meal was over Toby washed the dishes, before running back upstairs to his room. Taking each clock part individually, he cleaned them until they gleamed like new. As he finished polishing the last one, his Mother called up "you had better clean your teeth now love. It's nearly time for bed."

Looking over at his bedside clock, he saw that it was nearly nine o'clock, and he couldn't believe that the time had flown by so quickly. Suddenly feeling sleepy, he packed the pieces carefully into an old shoe box, and by the time he'd cleaned his teeth and got into bed, his parents came in to say goodnight. In normal circumstances as soon as the house was quiet, Toby would return to his nocturnal repair work, but feeling exhausted, he slipped straight off to sleep.

Waking early the next morning, he found that it was only six fifteen. Settling back down, he tried to go back to sleep, but couldn't. "It's that flipping clock" he murmured. So whilst his parents still slept he put it back together and cleaned it thoroughly. He was pleasantly surprised at the clocks transformation from a dirty old thing, covered in years of grime to a quality timepiece that was in almost pristine condition. Standing it on the bedside cabinet, he hoped that his Dad would decide to keep it now that it looked so much better. Taking the large brass key he wound it up once more but was surprised when it still didn't work. Disappointed by this latest setback, he studied it closely. Because he couldn't think of any reason why it wouldn't work. He was still sat there in silence. When his Mum called up, "Toby it's nearly time for school."

"Okay" he replied "I'll be down in a minute." Quickly showering he dressed and ran downstairs. Still baffled, he placed the clock carefully upon the kitchen dresser so that his Dad could see it when he came home. He soon found out that he wasn't the only one that was puzzled, as his Mother was puzzled too, at only having to only call him once. As he sat eating his breakfast in silence, she asked him "what's up, more problems at school?"

"Schools fine" he lied, suddenly remembering that he still had the distinct possibility of trouble looming with Roland.

"Well?" she said waiting impatiently for an answer.

"It's that clock, it still won't go" he moaned.

She smiled, "why worry about something like that. You always fix them in the end don't you?"

Realising that she was right again as usual Toby left for school, after the customary inspection and dreaded soppy wet kiss. Reaching class safely, and seeing that Roland wasn't present, he relaxed a little as he tried concentrating on the morning lessons of geography and religious education. However, he soon found his thoughts returning to the old clock.

Again, in the afternoon his mind continued to wander until a peeved Mr Montgomery, catching him daydreaming for the second time, shouted sarcastically. "Mr Smith if you listen to what I am saying, you may just learn something."

Toby tried hard to pay attention, but found that he couldn't. So, at the end of a very unproductive day, he ran as fast as he could towards home still thinking about what to try next with the infuriating clock. As he ran around the corner he bumped straight into Roland, who was with two older boys.

"Look what I caught" the bully squealed in delight as he grabbed Toby by the ear and pulled it hard. The other two boys, who were leaning against the wall, laughed. They hadn't forgotten that it was Toby's Mother who had reported them for stealing in the town centre some months earlier.

"Give him a good slap" one of them said spitefully as he took a long drag on his cigarette.

"Yeah, teach the little grass a lesson." The other boy added cruelly, with a nearly toothless snarl.

"Oooooh! Let me go" Toby yelled, as his ear throbbed painfully.

Howling with laughter, Roland yanked it all the harder. As he pulled his victim around the pavement shouting "you're gonna get it good now Jugs!"

Between laughing, the first boy asked stupidly. "Why do you call him Jugs?"

Roland replying spitefully "because his name's Toby of course. Plus he got these lovely sticky out ears. Get it now? Toby Jugs."

"Which look pretty sore to me" the second boy added.

Toby began crying, and he begged Roland to stop.

But urged on by his friends, Roland kept tugging for all he was worth.

"Let me go!" Toby screamed "or I'll tell."

"Tell who you little sissy" Tubs mocked "who's gonna save you this time?"

"I am" the answer came as Mr Raven stopped on his push bike.

"Not you again" Roland yelled. "Quick lads, leg it!" Without being told twice his friends ran off leaving an overweight Roland lagging behind.

Leaning his bike against the pavement curb, Mr Raven walked over asking "are you okay?"

Rubbing his ear, Toby answered "yes Sir, I think so."

The teacher frowned as he watched the three bullies disappearing into the distance.

"That's twice you've saved me now" Toby said gratefully "I dread to think what would have happened if you hadn't come along when you did."

"It was lucky for you that I did then, wasn't it" the teacher laughed. "I only came this way to get my watch repaired in the high street."

"I'm glad your watch is broken" Toby stated. Then, realising what he'd said he added quickly "I don't really mean that I'm glad it's broken, but I, I..."

Mr Raven interrupted him at once. "It's okay, I know what you mean."

Toby was relieved, and his face clearly showed it. "What's wrong with your watch?" he asked.

"If I knew that I'd repair it myself" Mr Raven replied, laughing.

Toby laughed too, as he was starting to feel a little better. "I could look at it for you if you like Sir?" he suggested.

"Why, do you know something about watch repairs?" The teacher asked, looking surprised.

“It’s my hobby” Toby replied enthusiastically. “I like repairing things.”

Mr Raven hesitated, “well I don’t know because this watch is a family heirloom.”

Surprising himself with how forward he was, Toby found himself shouting. “If I can’t fix it, I doubt anyone can.”

Agreeing to let Toby take a look at it, Mr Raven suggested that he took Toby home and met his parents at the same time.

Toby’s Mother was not at all happy at first about seeing her son with a stranger.

Finding out that he was a teacher from his school. She was relieved, although then fearful that her son had been misbehaving. After being assured that this was not the case, she insisted that Mr Raven stayed for tea. Accepting her offer at once, Mr Raven chatted with Toby in the kitchen. While his Mrs Smith busied herself preparing the evening meal.

After tea Toby took Mr Raven’s watch up to his bedroom, and after making a few minor adjustments, had it ticking like new. He hurried back downstairs with it immediately.

“That’s marvellous” Mr Raven exclaimed, offering to pay for the work done. Toby wouldn’t hear of it of course, but was very pleased that he had been able to repay the teacher for his kindness. As he was about to leave Mr Raven spotted the old clock on the dresser. “What a lovely old clock, who owns it?” he asked.

"My Dad" Toby replying instantly. But it doesn't work at the moment."

"No luck repairing it yet?" Mr Raven asked inquisitively.

Toby looked at the teacher's face, seeing the strange red light in his eyes again. Backing away, he responded warily "no, no luck yet," as he opened the door and ushered him into the sitting room.

Seeing Mr Smith, drinking tea the teacher immediately approached him and introduced himself, "Thomas Raven, history."

Standing up Mr Smith responded courteously "nice to meet you."

As they shook hands, the teacher suddenly asked. "That clock in the kitchen, do you want to sell it?"

Mr Smith smiled answering "why are you interested?"

"I'll make you a very reasonable offer" the teacher suggested.

Moving between the two men, Toby tried to interrupt their conversation. "Dad I haven't finished repairing it yet."

Ignoring him, Mr Raven took his Father by the arm. "Look I'll give you a hundred pounds if I can take it now."

Mr Smith's eyes lit up at the prospect of an unexpected windfall. He agreed at once, "yeah it's a deal."

Delighted by his success, Mr Raven got out his wallet and started counting out the money.

Toby continued protesting to his father. "But you promised me that I could repair it before you sold it."

His Father smiled and put his hand upon his shoulder. "I know I did son, and I'm sorry that I said that now. But some opportunities only come around once. You understand that don't you?" Rubbing his hands together he turned his attention back to the teacher who was holding out five twenty pound notes.

Mrs Smith who had been quietly watching from the kitchen, coughed to attract her husband's attention. "I thought that a promise was binding in this house" she said angrily.

Toby's father's eyes immediately lost their sparkle as he saw the money disappearing straight back down the drain. Sighing loudly he declared in a somewhat deflated tone. "I suppose you are right Martha. Our Toby can finish mending the clock. Mr Raven can always buy it after, if he still wants to?"

The teacher, who could see his prize slipping away, intervened and upped the ante immediately. "If you let me take it as it is, I'll pay you two hundred."

"Sorry" Mr Smith responded, sounding even more disappointed. "My wife's right, a promise is a promise."

"Well how much do you bloody want for it?" the distraught teacher shouted in frustration. Now, Stanley Albert Smith was an extremely tolerant man who was forgiving of most things, in most circumstances. However he was not so forgiving as to be spoken to like that in his own house. Gripping the teacher's arm firmly, he led him to the front door and easing him outside he whispered quietly "thank you for helping our lad out earlier, but the clock's not for sale any more, goodnight." Walking back into the sitting room, he heard the shocked teacher shout desperately "what about three hundred?"

Ignoring the increased offer, Mr Smith sat down in his favourite armchair by the roaring fire. "Boy he wants that clock pretty badly."

"He certainly does" his wife agreed "he was quite rude about it as well. He seemed like such a nice man earlier."

Leaving his Mum and Dad still discussing Mr Raven, Toby carried the old clock back upstairs to his bedroom and turned on his portable television just as a confused Dr Watson demanded "what do you mean by that Holmes?" Toby watched mesmerised as Sherlock Holmes the worlds greatest known detective replying with his usual dead pan face, responded confidently "after you rule out all the possible solutions it's only logical to consider the impossible ones." Toby turned the television back off instantly and focused his attention on the three spare cogs wondering if they too, somehow fitted into the old clock. He knew that there was nothing mechanically wrong with it, in the normal sense. So it should be working, but it wasn't. If Holmes's deduction was correct, perhaps something was wrong with it in the abnormal sense. If that really made any sense at all? After experimenting and getting nowhere for a couple of hours, he finally drifted off to sleep.

Awoken sometime later by a strange creaking noise. At first, he just lay there trying to work out exactly what it was. Suddenly realising that someone was trying to force open his bedroom window, he became quite afraid. Fortunately, with the thick velvet curtains drawn tight, whoever it was that was outside couldn't see in. However, because of the strong moonlight behind, Toby could see a tall dark silhouette. Shaking like a leaf, he slid quietly out of bed and crept in to wake his Dad, who after gathering his wits and his favourite golf club, hid in the corner of the partially illuminated bedroom in only his vest and pants. The window suddenly giving way with a loud crash. The hapless intruder was sent flying into the bedroom along with a shower of broken glass. Quickly untangling himself from the curtains, he cursed under his breath as he got to his feet.

Acting impulsively Mr Smith ran at him, and hitting him hard he sent him straight back through where the window used to be.

"Aghrrr!" The burglar screamed as he landed in the garden with a loud thud! Pulling himself up onto his feet again, he gingerly limped off into the darkness.

Reacting fast, Toby's Dad ran downstairs to give chase still waving his beloved sand wedge.

Returning sometime later, sweaty and panting breathlessly. Mr Smith wheezed “he got away on a bicycle. Crikey, I must have chased the blighter for miles.”

While he carried on giving his wife a more detailed account of the chase. Toby made them all a strong cup of tea to calm their nerves. After Mr Smith had finished his tea he said ominously. “I know it was dark and I can’t be sure but I think that the burglar was that teacher, Raven.”

Responding with the gift of hindsight, Mrs Smith nodded in agreement. “Well he was really upset about not buying the clock.”

“He sure was” Mr Smith agreed as a twinkle returned to his eye. “Maybe it is valuable after all” he chuckled. “He did offer me three hundred pounds for it and that’s a lot of money for a broken clock.” Rubbing his hands together, he added as an afterthought. “When we call the police in the morning I think that I just might mention Mr Raven to them.” Still smiling about a possible windfall he went upstairs to fix the broken window while Toby’s Mum cleaned up the broken shards of glass. After tucking Toby back in, they headed off to bed. As the bedroom door was closing Toby heard his Mother say proudly “you’re my hero Stanley.”

His Dad, who was obviously just a little bit embarrassed by the whole affair. Replied “don’t start that nonsense woman.”

Unfortunately, no matter how he tried Toby couldn’t go back to sleep. He feared that the intruder might return although he knew that the window had been nailed firmly shut. The one thing that really disturbed him though, was that his dad thought that Mr Raven might be the burglar. Toby wasn't so sure, for in the few seconds that the man had been in his room, he thought that it could have been just about anybody. At least his Dad was safe and that was the main thing. He could have just as easily have fallen out the window, as the intruder had done. The idea suddenly popping into his head that the thief may have been after the clock, he picked up his torch to look at it, just as a full moon was emerging from behind a dark rain cloud. Highlighting something engraved on the inside of the half open door. Shining his torch on the marks to get a better look at them, they disappeared only to mysteriously reappear as he aimed the beam of light away. Sussing out that the marks only showed up in lunar light, he angled the inside of the door towards the polythene covered window so that they could receive the maximum amount of moonlight possible. He gasped as the markings clearly showed how to reconfigure the clocks complicated mechanism. Gazing skywards at the full moon, he hoped that she wouldn't disappear back behind another cloud until he could make the necessary alterations. Working as fast as he could he followed the secret diagram step by step. As each piece fitted back into the clock in such a way, which never seemed either practical or possible. Persevering, he followed the detailed instructions until at last it was finished, and to his utter amazement he found that he had also used the three spare cogs as well. His heart pounding, he spun it around to see if it was going. Seeing the second hand moving, albeit slowly, his face lit up as he yelled "yippee" aloud in triumph forgetting momentarily that it was the middle of the night and his parents were still sleeping. Fortunately though, after all the excitement of earlier, they both were thoroughly exhausted and never heard him cry out. "Thank goodness" he whispered as he set the alarm, and feeling like the cat that ate the cream, fell soundly asleep.

Chapter Two
Grain Sandy Sea Bottom

Hearing the alarm, Toby turned it off and went into the bathroom where he took a quick shower and dressed. As he went back into his bedroom he noticed an eerie white light coming from the clock. Moving closer, he leaned over it to see what was causing it. The light suddenly becoming brighter, Toby felt rather frightened but before he could move back, he felt himself being drawn towards it. Struggling, he tried to break free but found that the unseen force was just too strong. "Help!" He yelled in panic, but no sound came from his quivering lips. It was if he'd been suddenly struck dumb. Still screaming silently, he was pulled right into the clock. "Ouch!" He shouted as he landed on his backside with a bump. Instead of being in his bedroom though, he was on a sandy beach. Looking up and down in bewilderment he studied the long golden shoreline but couldn't see anyone in either direction. He stared at the blood red ocean's foaming surf as it relentlessly crashed upon the deserted seashore in a constantly changing kaleidoscope of colours. "Crikey!" he exclaimed, noticing that the sky overhead was jet black. Although it was still clearly daytime. He looked up at the silver stars as they shimmered brightly like a billion twinkling diamonds. As the realisation suddenly came that he was just a tiny speck of dust, lost in the vast universe, a gruff voice suggested thoughtfully "stunning aren't they?"

Jumping up, Toby looked around, but couldn't see anybody. Deciding that he must have imagined it he sat back down, until the voice enquired impatiently. "Well young man are you going to answer me or not?"

He looked around again, still not seeing anybody.

"Not very bright is he?" a second voice observed, in a slightly higher pitch.

As a deep rumbling one added with a little more understanding. "Give him a chance, he looks lost."

Toby admitted freely "yes, I am lost and pretty confused because I can't see where you are hiding." His words greeted by mischievous laughter, Toby shuffled his feet nervously.

The first voice that had spoken grumbled miserably. "Hey, take your foot out of my eye."

Looking down at his feet, Toby's mouth dropped opened in surprise as he saw that he was standing upon a large grinning face.

"Flipping heck!" he exclaimed as he stumbled backwards and tripped over onto the soft golden sand.

"Keep still, you're hurting us" a squeaky voice cried desperately.

Remaining motionless he saw other faces appearing all around him but he couldn't help jumping up with fright as one suddenly popped up right between his legs. Panicking he ran along the beach screaming. Every time his foot came down upon the warm sand it was accompanied by an agonising cry of "Ahh!" Oohh!" or "Grr!" Realising that he was causing distress he stopped, shouting "I hope no one's too badly injured?"

"No were all fine, thank you." Yet another voice answering gratefully.

Still concerned, Toby asked "are you sure you're all okay? Where can I put my feet so that I don't hurt you?"

"Anywhere you like" a face nearby responded cheerfully. "We were only having a little bit of fun with you. You couldn't really hurt us, if you ran about all day."

"Thank goodness for that" Toby cried, feeling relieved. "I'm Toby Smith, who are you?"

The smiling face in the sand replied instantly "I'm Shell weed and I'm pleased to meet you." His cheek rippling gently, a small hand emerged from it.

Taking it cautiously, Toby shook it apprehensively. As a deep gravely voice behind him coughed and asked politely "excuse me, can I have a word?"

Turning around, he saw yet another face which was considerably larger than the others. He watched it curiously, as it beckoned him nearer using a small finger protruding from its left eye.

"Come over and sit down here next to me so we can talk properly" it rasped. "Grain Sandy Sea Bottom is my full name but you may call me Grain if you wish."

Toby walked over carefully and sat down next to the sand face noticing that he looked much older than the others. Although all the faces looked the same at first glance, on closer inspection they were all slightly different in either size, shape or texture. Their only identical feature being their sandy colour, which was uniform. So, with his head still reeling from being forcibly forced into an old clock, he sat down beside the face in the sand called Grain. For although his Mother had always told him not to talk to strangers she had never included friendly sand faces in her warnings. "I'm Toby Smith" he said politely, introducing himself.

"That's better, now we can talk properly" the kindly old face said as he smiled and asked "which sector are you from?"

Toby scratched his chin, responding shyly "I'm not from any sector that I know of, I'm from England."

Grain hesitated momentarily as he tried to place the name, England. He knew that it sounded vaguely familiar. "England, England, now let me see. England, yes I've heard of that place.

That's one of the places that old Seaple used to tell me about when he used to go off travelling all the time." Changing the subject, he said proudly. "This lovely place is called beach world."

Toby looked puzzled, "sorry" he said. "I've never heard of beach world. Is there a phone around here because I need to call my parents?"

Hurt by Toby's apparent lack of knowledge about his home. Grain demanded "surely you've heard of beach world? We are one of the oldest planets in the universe after all." He hesitated, waiting for an explanation. Not receiving one, he proclaimed proudly. "It's lovely here isn't it, and the beach goes on for several hundred thousand miles. Halting in mid flow, he asked "what's a phone?"

Toby began crying as the realisation suddenly hit home that he was really lost and this wasn't just a dream where he was going to wake up in his own bed. As tears started falling he shouted "look Mr Grain I don't know where I am or how I am going to get back home."

Forming a golden arm, Grain put it around Toby's shoulder saying softly. "Now, now there's no need for all that bawling is there."

Not responding to the friendly sandman, Toby became inconsolable.

"Please don't cry" the sandman asked again hopefully but no matter how much he pleaded, Toby just kept weeping.

Taking the shape of what roughly resembled a helicopter; Grain took off and hovered above the beach.

Taking no interest, Toby sobbed even louder.

Seeing no response from the youngster, the sandman climbed higher into the sky and performed a series of death defying loops before banking sharply and diving back towards the beach at breakneck speed.

Toby, who was by now watching enthralled, expected the helicopter to pull out at the last minute but accelerating, it crashed straight into the beach sending sand flying into the air in all directions. As the last few grains of sand drifted slowly down a soprano voice nearby shouted "that was great."

"It sure was," a husky voice agreeing quickly.

"Simply stunning," a third yelled.

One by one the other faces on the beach added their own comments of praise.

"Wonderful show " one shouted.

"Truly amazing" another confirmed.

"Staggering performance," still more declaring.

One lone voice in the distance crying out. "Well I didn't think he was that good." He was quickly drowned out as the sand dwellers calling for more.

Emerging from the beach in the form of a huge sandy bird, Grain climbed high into the sky again, and turning quickly he plummeted back down towards them. While his captivated audience gasped in anticipation and admiration. Levelling out, he dropped a large egg upon the lone dissenter, causing him to collapse. Then, skimming along the golden shoreline he effortlessly disappeared back into the beach, to reappear seconds later as a huge sharks fin.

Toby became anxious as it headed straight towards him. Until suddenly stopping, it became a lop eared rabbit on a pogo stick. Jumping up and down wildly, it tripped over its floppy ears and hit the beach hard. Exploding into hundreds of differently shaped butterflies who fluttering gracefully back to the beach, became Grain once more.

Cheering and whistling their approval, the noisy audience of sandmen clapped and waved while others forming huge fists, punched the air.

Toby watched the happy entertainer as he wallowed in their applause.

Winking at him the Sandman asked him quietly "did you like my performance?"

"Very much" Toby responded assuming that Grain was also pleased as his grin got considerably bigger. As all the noise and excitement gradually died down. Toby asked the shape changer "how do you do that?"

His face changing from a smile to a frown Grain confessed "I don't really know because altering my shape is something that I do naturally. How I actually do it though, now that's another thing all together. To answer you as best as I can I suppose I just sort of become whatever I picture in my mind."

"I don't agree" shouted the argumentative trouble maker from earlier who had now reformed his shape. Grain suddenly wished that he hadn't said anything as all the other sand faces also started shouting out their opinions as well. The heated debate deteriorating into nothing more than a noisy hubbub with no one really being able to hear what anyone else was saying. Grain suggested that he and Toby went further up the beach so that they could talk in peace. Turning into a frog, he hopped athletically away, closely followed by Toby who thought that it was a good thing that Miss Blakelock wasn't here with such a handsome little amphibian being available. He was still giggling about his private joke when the sandy coloured frog croaked "right, now we can talk without being disturbed." Shooting out his long tongue automatically, he caught a fly and swallowed it. Burping, he licked his lips, saying in explanation. "Sorry about that, but when you assume a living creature's form and capabilities you sometimes develop their nasty habits as well." Winking with one of his bulging eyes, he added wickedly. "But it's something that you learn to live with because it's all part of being a sandman. Anyway let's not talk about me. Now that you've cheered up a bit, we have to decide what's best for you."

Toby immediately asked the frog "can you help me get back home?"

Not wanting to make Toby start crying again. Grain answered positively "I can't, but I think I know someone who can." Although he knew that there was a distinct possibility that the lost child would be stranded here for ever with the zone being a place of uncertainty and constant turmoil. His face becoming serious, he added. "If I tell you everything that I know about what's going on, we can take it from there." He tapped his fingers rhythmically, wondering where too start. After a short pause he said, "have you heard of the Stinger Queen?"

"Who's that?" Toby answered.

"She's an evil creature, half monster, half wasp, who wants to rule the Zone or the Solar System as you would probably call it. But my old friend Seaple will stop her, as he did her Father."

"Who's Seaple?" Toby enquired.

Grain smiled with satisfaction. "Only the wisest being in the whole zone."

"Wow," Toby gasped aloud "and you know him?"

"Know him," Grain responding indignantly, "we're old buddies."

Toby moved nearer, asking anxiously. "Is he the one that can help me get home?"

"I hope so" Grain responded, trying to sound confident.

"Yippee!" Toby shouted, "Let's go now, does he live far?" He stopped shouting, as he noticed Grain's worried expression. "What's wrong?" he asked.

"Nothing" Grain answered, "but don't build your hopes up too much, just in case." Seeing Toby's face drop, he quickly added, "there probably won't be a problem. But, as I haven't seen old Seaple for years, we can't take anything for granted."

Toby felt disheartened, but trying to remain upbeat he whispered quietly "okay."

The sandman could tell that he was still upset. Deciding to cheer him up, he started changing into his whole repertoire of amusing Zone creatures including six legged slug bugs from forax, a green eyed merzi monster of Zerox and several snaggle toothed mud dippers from the planet zed. Seeing that his entertainment was being ignored though, he stopped, saying apologetically “sorry, but you needed to know just in case of a hitch. After all there’s a lot going on in the zone at the moment”

Toby kicked a small sea shell, shouting angrily. “I don’t care about that; all I care about is going home.”

Disappointed by Toby’s sudden outburst Grain sucked air into his mouth, until his head exploded. Reshaping immediately, his usually friendly face had been replaced by a serious looking scowl. “Now look here” he shouted “this isn’t a game that they’re playing. If the Stinger Queen gains control of the gravity machine everybody in the universe will be enslaved.”

“Sorry” Toby said solemnly, suddenly grasping the seriousness of the situation. “Am I forgiven?”

Sighing loudly Grain nodded, saying “I suppose so. You are only young after all. But remember that this conflict involves everyone, including your family.”

“What do you mean?” Toby asked.

Grain looked away, avoiding his gaze. “Do you think that the old shrew will spare your home planet?” he whispered.

Toby gulped and was about to ask several more questions but seeing the grave look upon the old sandman’s face, he decided not to. Instead, he wandered off alone and sat watching the strange looking seabirds that were diving into the turbulent crimson ocean. As they bobbed back to the surface with fish in their long crooked beaks, he remembered that he'd had no breakfast. Hurrying back to Grain he asked him "can you rustle me up something to eat? Especially if we have to walk all the way to Seaple's."

Forming his mouth into a trumpet shape Grain called out "Long beach, Shore shift, Star shell and Pebble stone. Go into the sea and find something for our guest to eat, and be quick lads because we need to get going as soon as possible."

Responding at once to their elder's request the four young sandmen moved slowly toward the ocean in search of something suitable. One in the form of a lopsided centipede that was considerably larger than its earthly equivalent.

The second, as a shuffling caterpillar who had two huge eyes and hundreds of different sized legs. The other two were a mish-mash of half formed limbs, distorted heads and spiny feet. Toby watched the grossly misshapen bunch of misfits as they waded awkwardly out through the incoming waves, and tried not too laugh, but found that he just couldn't help it.

Grain frowned at first, but realising that Toby never really meant any harm he laughed mischievously as well. As his booming chuckle, which sounded like a boats hull scraping upon jagged rocks, echoed around the beach.

Toby said, between giggles "they're not very good at changing shape are they?"

"No, they're not" Grain replied. "Although I wasn't much better than them when I was their age but they will improve with time and practice." They were still chuckling together when the four young sandmen scurried back up the beach carrying a large seaweed covered shell. Placing it carefully at the Toby's feet, they stood back awaiting his approval.

Bending down Toby pulled back the thick layer of seaweed, to reveal an algae covered platter which held a collection of juicy fat worms and slimy sea slugs. "I can't eat those!" He shouted in disgust, turning away disappointed.

Mystified by his unexpected response Grain thanked the sandmen. "Sorry lads, but he doesn't seem to want them now so put the little wrigglers back into the ocean." As the disgruntled fisherman slowly trudged back into the foaming surf, Grain demanded frostily "I thought you were hungry?"

"I am" Toby exclaimed. "But I can't eat that kinda stuff, it's horrible."

Scratching his head, Grain smiled sympathetically. "How are we suppose know what you eat? You are from another zone after all, and I've never had anything to do with humans. The little bit I know about your species is what Seaple told me years ago."

Toby smiled, albeit not a very enthusiastic one. "Okay, I'm sorry that I shouted, but no more worms."

"That's a deal" Grain agreed, changing into the more comfortable form of a chimpanzee. "We had better be leaving now because it will take us several days to reach the secret door that leads into Seaple's world." Without waiting for an answer, he bounded away on all fours leaving Toby behind, struggling to keep up. After travelling for several miles Toby started wilting badly. Not noticing that he was struggling, Grain just kept on walking as he spoke of the old days and paddled his monkey feet in the cool sea. "Before Darvock came this was a good place to live as most of the species in the surrounding worlds were relatively peaceful." He closed his eyes, as he slowed his pace slightly. "Which is surprising as the diversity of creatures in the zone is absolutely staggering. For there are sea worshippers who live only on giant fish and hairy hunters who stalk savage beasts in dark jungle worlds. While others, like the nut men for example build houses in palm trees, living only on coconuts unlike the mole people live deep down in the earth, feeding voraciously on giant grubs." Grain stopped momentarily, and then continued as he got his second wind. "The list is simply endless and still growing as the zone continues to expand. There are the one eyed sun worshippers, hairy tree beasts, crab monsters and hole maggots. As well as chiller frillers and acid faced tongue wrigglers. That's just some of the more colourful ones that I've heard of for there are literally millions of others including wild tribes of head hunting pygmies who..." Stopping, he looked down casually expecting to see a wide eyed Toby walking at his side. His voice trailed off as he suddenly realised that he was alone. Swivelling his head around upon a stalk, he looked back along the beach and spotted Toby on his hands and knees. Quickly turning into a seven legged whizz cat he sprinted back and reached him in mere micro seconds. Sliding to a halt and creating a long furrow in the damp sand, he asked anxiously "are you ill?"

Toby, who was suffering badly with painful stomach cramps gripped his throbbing midriff tightly as he tried to cope with the searing bursts of pain. Mumbled desperately "if I don't get some food and fresh water I won't be able to carry on."

Seeing that his travelling companion was in a bad way Grain thought about what might be more suitable for him to eat than worms. Shouting "stay here, I'll be back soon" as he ran out into the breaking surf and turning into a large eel. He dived head first into the bubbling red ocean, leaving Toby still clenching his stomach.

Before Toby knew it, the sandy coloured eel slithered back out of the water and changing back into a chimpanzee. He loped up the beach with a wide grin upon his face. "Brrr! I'd forgotten just how enjoyable swimming can be" he said. "I shall have to try and do it more often in future." Crouching down beside Toby he said "here, try one of these." He opened up his fingers slowly, revealing four red berries cradled in his palm.

Toby eyed them hoping that they were something to eat. Taking them from Grain carefully he studied them. “What are they?” he enquired, wincing once more in agony.

“Sea cherries” the chimp replied.

Toby rolled one between his thumb and finger asking “are they edible?”

The chimp leaned nearer, “that’s the problem, I don’t know. But as they were eaten by several species long ago. I expect you can eat them as well. Although, until you actually try one, who knows? But after centuries of over harvesting, there’s only a few of them left now. Down really deep, in secret dark places. If you know where those places are, and you have the ability to become an eel, they’re still available.”

Toby licked one of the cherries with his tongue, finding it almost tasteless. “Shall I try one?” he asked.

Grain frowned, “like I said, I assume that you can eat them. But not being from this world, we can’t really be certain until you try one.”

Toby grabbed his stomach, as another sharp spasm of pain ripped through his stomach.

“Do you really have a choice?” Grain asked. Becoming a sand face, he added “I can tell you what was sung about them long ago,” as he began to sing:

“Dive deep, seek the cherries.
Quench your thirst, stop your hunger.
Fill the larder full of berries.
Feel pain no longer.”

"Make of them what you will.
All your heart desires.
Your need now fulfilled.
Put out the funeral pyres."

Toby was fascinated by the strange old song but his stomach rumbling violently again, it quickly brought him back to reality. "What does that actually mean" he gasped?

Grain grimaced, "if the old stories are true. They taste of whatever you think of."

That being good enough for Toby, he popped one straight into his mouth and started sucking furiously. He tried to imagine a double cheeseburger with fries on the side washed down with an ice cold cola and chocolate ice cream. Although he never believed for one moment that the sea cherry would actually work, straight away though he could taste the distinctive flavour of a cheeseburger quickly followed by hot French fries which even had lashings of salt and vinegar on them, just how he liked them. "Wow!" He exclaimed in excitement as the flavour started changing again. Closing his eyes he concentrated on the creamy chocolate ice cream that was running down his throat until it was replaced by the freezing cold cola. Burping contentedly he smiled at the old sand king who was laughing quietly to himself, "I assume it worked?" he asked.

"I should say so" Toby replied gratefully rubbing his bulging stomach. As he studied his greatly increased girth although he knew that he preferred looking a little plump, instead of having the awful stomach cramps. “I feel as if I could walk a thousand miles now” he said still rubbing his swollen pot belly with his small hands.

“I don’t think it will come too that” Grain replied. “But be careful about how you use the sea cherries, because it could be dangerous to use them too often. Keep them hidden and only use them in emergencies.”

Putting the three remaining cherries into his pocket, Toby just started thinking about a cup of steaming hot coffee when he heard a loud splash of water behind them. Turning around he saw several lime green coloured creatures that were soaring majestically into the air before returning to the water with a noisy crash! Strangely though, they only had one large red eye which was set in the middle of their foreheads. Sploosh! Went another large spray of water as the rest of the group saluted the acrobatics by hitting the water with their tails.

“Bravo!” Toby shouted, as each of the creatures took turns performing their spectacular trick. “What are they called Grain?” he asked.

Pretending not to notice them, the old sandman whispered quietly “they’re scooters. But don’t encourage them because they’re big headed, and all they ever want to do is show off. So it’s better if we just ignore them.” Stony faced, he strode away leaving the playful creatures still frolicking in the sea.

Catching him up, Toby asked “that’s a bit harsh isn’t it?”

"No, I don't think it is" Grain replied. "Because they never take anything seriously."

Before Toby could press any him further a hard jet of water hit the Grainster full in the face, sending him flying through the air. Landing heavily, he crumpled into a wet pile of soggy sand.

Toby looked down in horror to where his splattered pal lay, seeing a small mouth and solitary eye.

"Shhh" the mouth whispered quietly " I don't want those jokers to see me."

"Are you hurt?" Toby asked anxiously.

"Of course not " Grain replied with a wink. "I'm fine; I just don't want those stupid scooters ridiculing me again. You keep walking along the beach ignoring them while I keep out of sight." Changing into a long thin worm, he slipped down into the soft sand and wriggled along in cognitio.

Noticing that the Scooters were now keeping pace with him. Toby did as the sandman advised and said nothing.

Until the leading scooter casually enquired "is the grumpy old sand king sulking?"

This made Toby feel rather uncomfortable. For although Grain had said to ignore them, his parents had always taught him to be respectful to others unless they gave you a reason to do otherwise. Deciding that it probably wouldn't hurt to speak to them he answered politely. "Grain's not grumpy really; he's just got a lot on his mind."

The scooter smirked, using his two big red floppy lips. "Well he must have a lot of problems, because he's always serious. Why can't he lighten up a little?"

Toby waded out into the water until it was up to his knees. "Look friend" he said "if you can help us we'd be very grateful but if not, we'd appreciate it if you could leave us alone." He resumed walking, as the scooter pondered upon his words. Several hundred yards later, the scooter hailed him again.

"Yes," Toby replied.

"We'll see" the one eyed fish answered, and with a swish of his tail he was gone quickly followed by the others.

As soon as the coast was clear Grain emerged from the sand and took the form of a short squat lizard. Shooting out his forked tongue he hissed gratefully. "That was nice of you to defend me."

Toby smiled, "not a problem. Especially if you give me a ride."

The lizard stopped and looking at his companion he responded dryly "okay. But only if you promise not to eat too much."

Agreeing to Grain's request, Toby hopped onto his back asking "what's Seaple like?"

The lizard slowly plodded off, saying in thick guttural tones. "He took over the stewardship of the zone a long time ago but nobody knows where he came from originally.

Before he arrived here, life was far more dangerous than it is now as warring races constantly tried to conquer each other using the secret doors that connect all the worlds. He stopped all that of course, and we had peace for a long time until

Darvock's horde conquered the planet Alexis. As news of his decisive victory spread, others flocked to join him. The planets Fauna and Mestopheles fell soon after. That was when Seaple intervened, gathering all the life forms that he could muster. He attacked Darvock's army in the desolate waste of the Tiberg desert on the planet spiero.

After a bloody battle, lasting many days with thousands of soldiers falling on both sides. He and Darvock committed their remaining forces as they tried to secure a final victory. Now up to that point, I must admit that I never realised that they were both wizards. Not until they faced each other on the battle field." Grain hesitated as the memories of a brutal war came flooding back to him. Steeling himself, he continued in hushed, almost reverential tones, "The duel between them stood on a knife edge and it could have gone either way as they hurled flaming blue bolts of lightning at each other. After a terrible struggle, lasting several hours. Seaple eventually managed to overcome Darvock. Just as his victory was secured, darkness fell and Darvock slipped away in the chaos of battle." They stopped walking so slipping down off Grain's back, Toby sat on his long bumpy tail as the sandman whispered quietly "nobody escaped the horror of that terrible war."

Noticing that his cheeks were dark, Toby suspected that the shadowy patches under his eyes were tears. "Why does it still make you so sad when it was such a long time ago?" he asked.

"Old friends" Grain answered sadly. "Old friends who are now long gone. It brought everything flooding back, as we talked about the bad old days." He ambled off slowly, with Toby hot on his heels. Just as he was about to remount him, Grain turned back into a chimp and continued his sorrowful tale. "When the remnants of Darvock's army disbanded and went back to their homes we searched for him for months but he had disappeared without a trace. Rumours were rife about his whereabouts of course, but we never found him. Leaving old Seaple with his grand plans for rebuilding everything that had been destroyed, I headed back home to the beach along with all the other sandmen that had answered the call to arms. But, when we reached our home, there was a stranger there who seemed quite an amusing fellow to begin with. As he told his interesting stories and funny anecdotes all the other sandmen were captivated by him. I wasn't so sure about him myself as I always had the feeling that there was more to him than met the eye. As I'd not long returned from the war, I was probably less trusting than most because that's the kind of thing war does to you. Altering your values and perceptions of life.

As time passed, the thought came to me that he could be Darvock. Although I must confess to you that I'd never actually seen the wizard up close, deciding to err on the side of caution I told the other sandmen elders about my fears but they thought that I was just imagining it. Believing they were probably right I left him alone until a young sandman told me that as soon as the older sandmen were absent, he stopped telling tales of folklore and started telling tales of conquest. It was then that I knew for sure that I'd been right all along. Grain studied the young child beside him. Now we sandmen are a remarkably simple people who do not need much from life. Just a bit of beach with plenty of sun, sea and sand. It's a very basic existence, I know but that's the way we like it. The younger sandmen though, suddenly started wanting more from life so I approached the elder's again telling them that I had been correct about the stranger. As they were indecisive about what to do, I confronted him myself, growing to my full height I demanded that he left our world but he only laughed at me screaming "that I was just an old fool and that I had better go away."

Losing my temper, I attacked him immediately." Grain looked gaunt, as he recalled the grisly horror of that day. "Casting a spell, he sent me stumbling backwards. Hitting the floor hard I felt a tremendous weight bearing down on me, and I thought that I was going to shatter with the pressure. But he had badly misjudged the power of sandmen when they are threatened. Quickly joining together to form a long wall the other elders tried to push him off our beach but Darvock wasn't about to be beaten that easily. Casting another spell, he caused several of them to disintegrate. Unable to reform their shape again, they were lost forever. But as he concentrated his will upon them, he forgot about me, just for a split second, so forming a huge fist, I hit him hard killing him outright."

Toby felt sad for his friend, although he realised there was little he could do to comfort him. As real friends do in times of crisis, he decided to help in whatever way was possible, that being the least he could do for the big yellow guy. He tried raising Grain's spirits by changing the subject. "Do you have any children?" he asked.

Shaken out of his sombre mood, Grain responded jovially. "We do not have children in the way that most species do. We have what we sand dweller's call splits. That's when a small piece of us separates and develops into another small sandman." He smirked smugly, "I have several living in the community. Let me see now" he said, as he paused a moment to think. "Oh yes, I have seven in all. Shore twig, Sand shift, Wave tide, Surf star, Sandstorm Storm son and Windross. I will introduce you to them later, if we have the opportunity."

"Thanks, it would be great to meet your splits" Toby exclaimed, suddenly realising how much he was missing his Mum and Dad. He blurted out unintentionally "I wish that I could let my parents know that I'm safe."

Grain looked thoughtful, "look I can't promise anything" he said "but Seaple maybe able to arrange that for you if he can't get you back home immediately."

As the waning orange sun disappeared on the horizon, passing its rising brother, the unusual pair of friends kept moving towards the hidden door that led to Seaple's world. Becoming bored, Toby waded through the incoming waves while Grain constantly changed into different life forms to keep himself amused. Sometimes the shapes he took resembling animals that Toby recognised while at other times, the creatures looked nothing like anything that lived on Earth. Toby wasn't frightened though, because no matter how hideous the monsters looked he knew that it still the Grainster.

"Ouch!" Toby yelled as he walked straight into something hard and fell backwards onto the sand. Looking up, he couldn't see anything there. "What hit me?" he moaned rubbing his sore nose.

Ignoring him, while he concentrated. Grain who was now in the shape of a loose limbed gibbon started probing with his long nimble fingers looking for the secret lock that would allow them to pass into the next world. "It's here somewhere" he cried. "If only we can find it." He continued feeling around for the switch, which he knew was there somewhere. "Ooh, ahh, nearly" he said, as he began fiddling with something.

Toby put out his hand before him and touched the invisible door which divided the two worlds as Grain shouted ecstatically "got it!"

Chapter Three
Hero

Clambering through the open doorway into the next world, Grain glanced back at his homeland. Seeing thousands of waving hands that looked like a sea of golden daffodils. Responding with a broad smile, he bowed but as he closed the door, his face turned grave with worry.

Toby took his hand, saying "don't worry we'll both be back home soon."

Grain, who was feeling despondent about leaving his beloved beach world, only replying sombrely "I hope so." Leaving his friends behind they started walking across the immaculately manicured lawns which were planted with numerous blossoming trees and vast swathes of wild flowers.

Toby named the ones that he recognised. "That's a flowering cherry and this is a cut leaf maple. Oh and those over there are silver birch while these colourful little flowers by our feet are bluebells and daffodils." Stopping by an enormous black plant which had thick hairy leaves resembling long leathery red tongues, he asked curiously "what's that ugly thing called?"

"Get away from that now!" Grain shrieked. "That's a Tyrolean catcher plant and it eats virtually anything, including nosey children."

Jumping back quickly, Toby realised that he'd have to be more careful. "Thanks Grain" he said gratefully. "I didn't know that it was dangerous, as it's not from my world. But why are there so many plants here from Earth?"

Grain grinned, "that's Seaple for you. He never could resist collecting plants when he went travelling around the zone. That's why are so many here from different places. So don't touch anything unless you know what it is."

Taking the Sandman's advice, Toby avoided contact with anything for several miles until he spotted a large gnarled old tree which towered majestically over everything else surrounding it. "Blimey what a beauty he cried."

Grain, who was still thinking about home didn't hear him and kept walking.

Toby, who found the giant tree fascinating, examined its long green lancet shaped leaves and oddly shaped fruit which resembled large orange perforated pumpkins. Suddenly a stony hand gently gripping his shoulder he realised that the Grainster had noticed that he was missing and had come back. "This tree's unusual" Toby stated, putting one foot upon its enormously twisted root system.

Pulling him back off it firmly Grain answered sternly. “Let’s just leave that old whistle snorer alone in case it holds us up.”

“How?” Toby enquired waiting for a reply.

Seeing that the stubborn Earth child was going nowhere until his curiosity was satisfied. Grain sighed wearily at being asked yet another question. Smiling like an understanding Father to his Son he whispered quietly. “When the wind blows through its fruits it makes a high pitched whistling sound which puts anyone hearing it to sleep, until the wind stops. Which can be really inconvenient if you are trying to get somewhere in a hurry like us,” he added frostily.”

“Cool” Toby squealed, “so are we safe here?”

“We are” his impatient companion replied “unless a breeze suddenly picks up of course then we will stay here sleeping until it dies back down again. So, unless you have any other questions to ask, I suggest that we go now.”

Toby replied mischievously. “Questions, oh I’ve only got about another million.” Seeing his feeble attempt at humour only greeted with a wall of silence, he decided to keep quiet for a while as they skirted around the base of the giant tree.

Passing it without incident, they soon saw a large wood in the distance. Quickening their pace, they kept it up until they reached the forest edge. At first they made good progress through the sparsely planted trees but as they went deeper into the heart of the forest it became much more difficult. As the densely grouped trees competed for light and space while being continually strangled by thick layers of green moss and suffocating ivy. Toby thought back to his Dad at home when he used to trim the overgrown variegated ivy in their back garden. Although he was missing his parents considerably, he did his best to keep up with the versatile sandman to whom thick foliage and thorny brambles made little difference. Grain scurried along at ground level in the form of a mole like creature, but for Toby though, it was becoming almost impossible. He tripped over every twisted vine and root, and got snagged by every sharp thorn. But with his energy levels being maintained by numerous helpings of chocolate and fizzy lemonade, he battled on regardless, until an excited Grain shouted back, from somewhere up ahead. "Don't worry youngster, we should reach the mud track soon and if we're really lucky we'll catch some buzzers to ride." Then he started singing loudly.

"Buzzers, buzzers where are you found?
In hollow trees.
Or caves underground.

Buzzers, buzzers why do you hide?
Come furry little friends.
Tired travellers need a ride.

Buzzers, buzzers help us if you can.
Always busy buzzing.
Since time began.

Come friendly buzz bomb.
Do what you do.
If I grab your mane or tail.
Can I ride with you?"

Still humming to himself he slipped agilely under the last of the thorny branches until he reached the brown muddy path in the middle of the forest. "Lovely spot for an ambush" he said slyly to himself, changing into a large hooded snake.

When Toby came crashing through the foliage a little later, he tripped over the reptile's out stretched tail and was sent flying through the air. Landing with a loud splat he sent mud flying in all directions as he slid to a halt. "Yuck!" He moaned bitterly as he wiped his dirty face.

Retracting his tail into the comparative safety of his folded coils. Grain hissed dryly "sssss try to be more careful."

"Yeah" Toby responded sarcastically. "But if you never left your tail in the flipping way it would help." Dragging himself up onto his knees he sat there, covered in mud watched by the still grinning snake, who hissed with amusement. "I love it; it's good for the complexion."

"That maybe the case for a reptile, but I don't like it much" Toby answered miserably. "What's this blimming track used for anyway?" It's far too slippery for people to walk on?"

Cocking his head to one side the giant snake hissed again. He flicked out his long tongue, tasting the air. "Sss, not so loud" he said, buzzers use this track as a shortcut through the forest. If we can catch a couple, we can ride them all the way to the castle saving us a few days of hard walking and lots of time." His eyes suddenly darting to one side, he listened intently, adding. "Quick, get out of sight and be ready for the ride of your life. I think I can hear some of them coming this way now."

Slipping back into the thick green foliage. Toby waited with bated breath to see what manner of beast that they were aiming to catch.

Grain slid silently down deeper into the welcoming mud. "Shhhhh, they're getting close" he whispered. "Oh and by the way," he added with a wink. "On my signal grab one by the tail or mane and what ever you do, don't let go." Submerging deeper into the muddy water he left only his nostrils and eyes showing, and then closing his scaly eye lids, he disappeared altogether.

Toby tensed with apprehension and anticipation as three oddly shaped creatures came slowly into view. Coming within a few yards of where they were hiding, the funny looking creatures hesitated, as if they suspected danger. But, after a short discussion, they proceeded cautiously. Toby looked down to where Grain was concealed as the buzzers got closer. Sniffing the air the wary creatures became agitated once more as they deliberated about whether it was safe to go on or not. Eventually, after deciding that it was clear, they accelerated forward at speed. Suddenly the wily old Sand king whipped out his tail and sent them all spiralling out of control into the forest where they became entangled in the dense foliage. “Yahoooo!” Grain shouted ecstatically as he slithered out from his hiding place and changed into a chimpanzee. Leaping nimbly aboard the nearest floundering animal, he held on tight. The buzzer, who suddenly felt the weight of an unwanted passenger, immediately increased its effort to break free. Buzzing louder than ever, it flapped its two large transparent wings powerfully as it frantically fought for its freedom. Finally breaking loose, of its bonds it shot straight up through the dense forest canopy, with Grain still aboard.

Toby, who had been rooted to the spot watching the bizarre spectacle, suddenly realised that he was in real danger of being left behind. Somewhat apprehensively he approached the second buzzer but found that he couldn’t mount it because of its rapidly beating wings. As he hesitated awaiting a chance to clamber aboard, it suddenly became untangled and sped away. Turning to the last beast that was still caught in the undergrowth, Toby ran over and leapt straight onto its hairy back.

Reacting instantly to his presence, the creature reared and bucked violently as it tried to dislodge him. Dragging himself further up the animals back. Toby grabbed hold of its wiry black mane as it bucked and kicked wildly beneath him. “Buzzzzzzzzzzzzzzzzzz” it wailed in a deafening high pitched whine. Breaking free, it accelerated straight up into the blue sky above. Flipping over, it flew upside down while a screaming Toby held on grimly for his life. With gravity inevitably taking over, he reluctantly let go and was sent plummeting down towards the ground below. "Noooooooooo!" He screamed as he hurtled down towards the rapidly growing fir trees. Just as the fast approaching ground seemed like it was close enough for him to touch, the buzzer slipped beneath him and caught him gently upon his back. Apparently, unconcerned about his near fatal fall, the strange creature grinned, asking cordially "where to?"

Shocked by what had just taken place and at the creature's ability to speak Toby nearly fell off his back again. Recovering his balance and composure quickly he took a tighter hold of the thick flowing black mane and stammered timidly "you can talk."

"Of course I can talk" the buzzer responding indignantly. "I was top buzz of my year actually."

"Good" Toby replied automatically and after taking a deep breath he added "I'm Toby, who are you?"

Looking back at him, the buzzer winked comically and yelled cheerfully. "I'm Beearney, but call me Barn, because everyone else does. Oh and I hope I wasn't too rough when I shook you free just now but that's how it works with us buzzers. If you're ever lucky enough to catch one, it's tradition that I buck you off and optional whether I catch you again."

Toby was relieved that Beearney had decided to retrieve him again. So, feeling just a little bit more secure upon his new mode of transport, he studied the funny creature beneath him with great interest. His black and yellow striped body was approximately four feet long and rather bee shaped. But, unlike bees back at home, his head and legs were more horse like. Toby patted his thick hairy neck gently saying politely “thank you for catching me but I’d be even more grateful if you could take me to see someone called Seaple.”

With another friendly wink the buzzer changed direction and headed towards Seaple’s castle. Toby relaxed and enjoyed the beautiful rugged wilderness below. He saw its clear crystal blue lakes and fast running rivers which ran through many dark green valleys, surrounded by tall craggy blue mountains.

After several hours of flying, they came to the end of the rugged mountain range. Cutting his speed the happy buzzer glided down between the last snow capped peaks, and skimmed confidently over the giant green conifers below.” Not long now” he shouted back.

Toby nodded in gratitude, but was glad that the journey was coming to an end as he was starting to feel rather saddle sore. Before he could dwell on his growing discomfort too long, a burning ball of yellow flame hurtled past them with a noisy whoosh! “What’s going on” he shouted? As the buzzer started rapidly climbing again. Realising that they were under attack and veering sharply left and right, he dodged another ball of flame. While his frightened passenger held on by his fingertips. Whoosh! Went another searing hot fireball, exploding just above their heads.

While Toby tried to try to see who was firing at them, Beearney was violently hit in the side by yet another flaming projectile. “Bzzzzzzzzzz” he screamed aloud in pain as he burst into flame and hurtled down towards the ground. Spotting a small clearing below, he gritted his teeth and extended his burning wing out painfully. Belly flopping into the tall green summer grass they slid at speed towards the oncoming trees ahead. Digging in his hooves and they slithered to a juddering halt!

Jumping off straight away Toby put out the few remaining embers of smouldering fire, and realising that the buzzer was severely hurt he took his head carefully in his hands and whispered “how are you fella?”

Beearney tried to stand, but couldn’t. He opened his big blue bulbous eyes, mumbling weakly “sorry. But I don’t think that I’ll be able to take you the rest of the way now.”

Tears welling up in the corner of his eyes, Toby stemmed them defiantly, demanding “how can I help?”

Again the buzzer tried to rise, but he was too weak. Managing to lift his head he groaned in barely more than a whisper. “You can’t, only the sap from a healing treacle tree can save me now.” He called upon his fast fading strength adding sadly “but there isn’t one for a hundred miles.”

Putting Beearney’s head back down upon the ground gently. Toby looked at his injury, seeing that the ragged gash in his side was deep. Taking off his school jacket, he pressed it against the seeping wound trying to stem the flow of luminous pink blood. Not really having much effect, he tried thinking of something else. Remembering the sea cherries, he quickly took one from his pocket and gazed into the buzzer's half closed eyes, yelling "quick swallow this."

The buzzer not responding, Toby yelled in desperation "come on Barn because I'm not going to let you die on me." Tilting his head back gently he pulled his mouth open and tossed the cherry right in, while massaging his throat gently. "Come on, swallow it" he pleaded.

Murmuring softly, Beearney gulped swallowing the cherry.

Toby prised open his eyes open a little wider as he tried to make him to understand what he wanted him to do. "Think of the sap from the treacle tree" he implored him. "Think of it now."

Closing his eyes, Beearney became still.

"Noooooo!" Came the anguished cry from Toby. Falling to his knees he pounded the ground in utter frustration. He stared down at the stricken buzzer in despair and then saw him twitch, and then twitch again.

Opening his eyes Beearney smiled weakly as he grew a little stronger. "Wow what was that you gave me?" He whispered "I feel a little better already."

"Yes, yes, yessssss!" Toby yelled as new skin start growing rapidly over the charred open wound. He also thought that the buzzer had also gained a few extra pounds as well. But, before he could remark about his new friend's portly appearance, he heard an angry voice bellow angrily "over this way stupid."

Putting a finger quickly to his lips he indicated the need for silence.

Beearney nodded, signifying that he understood. Slipping quietly into the safety of the nearby bushes they waited to see who had been firing at them.

"Not there, here somewhere" the irritated male voice yelled.

"Coming Sir," a second voice answered breathlessly.

Toby watched as Mr Raven entered the small clearing, closely followed by a red faced Roland who stopped only yards away from where they were hiding. The agitated teacher, who was carrying a thick walking stick, scanned the undergrowth. Spotting that Roland had sat down, he ordered angrily. "Well go and search for them because they've got to be around here somewhere."

Ignoring the teachers request Roland stayed where he was until Raven saw him and rebuked him mercilessly. "Get up and find them you fat fool. If they get away I'll skin you alive."

Without answering him, Roland got up and started looking around while muttering unhappily under his breath.

Beearney nudged Toby's shoulder gently and whispered quietly. "If we stay here they will find us eventually. Let's make a break for it while we still can."

Nodding silently, Toby slipped quietly onto his back and held on tight. The rejuvenated buzzer accelerated out from their hiding place.

Seeing them almost at once, Raven swung at them wildly, but missed. Roland caught Beearney on the side of head with a large rock which sent him crashing into an old tree trunk and Toby into a thick patch of tall hairy plants.

"Go in and drag him out boy" Raven screamed.

Following the teacher's order Roland searched the undergrowth. Spotting Toby's bright red hair he yanked him out roughly crying "here's the little ginger nut!"

Raven grinned like a fox that had just caught a chicken. "Well, well, look what we've caught." He cooed sadistically as he grabbed Toby forcefully by the shoulder. "And so very young to suffer such a nasty accident. Unfortunately though, that's the way it goes." He stared directly into the frightened boy's face. "It could have been different if only you had let me buy that clock. It would have prevented you coming here. But no, you had to keep it for yourself and make me look stupid." Tightening his grip upon Toby, he strode off through the trees leaving Beearney unconscious, and Roland bringing up the rear. As they emerged out of the cool shade of the forest into the warmth of the sunshine, Raven stopped and stared down into a deep ravine. "Wow that's a long way down" he said as he nonchalantly kicked a small stone over the edge. Grabbing Toby with both hands he tried to throw him over.

“Noooooooooo!” He screamed as he grabbed a hold of the teacher’s coat.

Laughing maniacally, Raven ignored his plea for mercy as he tried to shake his unwanted burden loose.

Roland watched what was happening, but couldn’t believe what he was seeing. Gathering his wits, he rushed forward and tried pulling his classmate back to safety. “What are you doing?” He shouted angrily “you never said anything about hurting him.”

Ignoring his protest Raven hit him hard, sending him flying backwards.

Turning his attention back to his captive he tried prising him free again. Which was proving difficult, as Toby fought for his life with the tenacity that only impending doom brings. Again and again Raven pulled his tiny fingers free only for him to lock himself onto him somewhere else. Striking his victim with a clenched fist, he raised him aloft in triumph and threw him over.

“Agrhhhhh!” Toby screamed as he clawed the air. He tried to grab hold of something to stop him from falling but found nothing but rushing air. He plummeted towards the jagged rocks below. “Ow!” He yelped, as something hard suddenly poked him hard in the back. “Ow!” He cried again as the treatment was repeated. “Ow! Ow! Ow! He yelled, as he was hit several more times in quick succession. Craning his neck around, he saw thousands of old twisted roots which were shooting out from the cliff face, trying to slow him down. Numb with shock and paralysed with fear, he passed out.

Toby awoke sometime later safely upon the ground. At first he just lay there, reliving his last conscious moments. Realising that the roots had saved him he reached out and stroked one of them saying courteously “thank you for saving my life. Without you’re help I’d surely have been killed.” Then in a moment of spontaneous gratitude he kissed the gnarled earth covered root gratefully adding “and if I can ever repay you I will.” The nearest root shook ferociously, so Toby started moving back. It grabbed his leg, preventing him from doing so taking an even tighter grip on his ankle, held him securely. All the other roots, coming alive once more, reached out to touch him as well. But as soon as they had made contact with him, they retracted back into the rock face only to be replaced by others who also wanted to touch him. Now although Toby wasn’t really sure what was going on, he never felt in danger at any time because these roots had just saved his life. He guessed that there was no point them doing that if they wished him any harm. He had to admit though, that it was a little bit scary all the same. Eventually after every root had touched him and had returned back into the cliff, the living manacle gently slipped from his ankle setting him free. Slipping out of the solid rock one by one, the roots slithered down the sheer rock to form a huge seething mass of writhing twigs. He watched them as they intertwined and slowly shaped themselves into a huge quivering ball. The ball kept growing bigger and bigger, until every last knotty twig had joined.

Toby watched the transformation of all the roots into one single entity. He jumped a mile, as the excited root ball suddenly shouted ecstatically. “Free, we’re free at last.” It started bouncing up down, enjoying its new found freedom. Settling down quickly, it rolled over and stopped in front of the gob smacked child asking “thanks, who are you?”

Toby smiled broadly at the root ball who was using a small gap between two of its roots as a make shift mouth. “I’m Toby Smith” he answered timidly.

The root ball, while resisting the desire to bounce said “I’m Rooter and I want to thank you for releasing me from Darvock’s spell.”

Putting out his tiny hand before him Toby grinned, and saying the first thing that come in his head he responded. “I’m glad I could help you, especially after you saved me.”

Forming several twigs into a make shift limb the root ball took his hand and shook it firmly saying “a pleasure, a real pleasure. It’s been such a long since that wizard imprisoned us here. He mocked us, saying that we would remain here forever unless we were released by an innocent child’s love.” I remember how he laughed as he walked away saying coldly. “But what child will ever love a bunch of dirty old sticks?” Although we lived in hope that someone would release us one day, we never really expected it to ever happen of course.

Now that you have broken his spell and released us we are eternally grateful."

Toby sat down and smiled at the ball of roots ruefully. "Grateful, but you just saved my life for Pete's sake."

Rooter grinned "that's all well and good. But if there is anything that we can ever do for you, never be afraid to ask."

"That's a deal" Toby said as a battered looking Beearney landed beside them.

"Are you okay?" he asked as he greeted Toby with a great big hug.

"I'm fine" Toby squealed, delighted to see the friendly buzzer again.

"How did you get all the way down here?" Beearny asked, looking puzzled.

"Raven threw me over, but Rooter saved me."

"Thank goodness for that" Beearney declared.

Knowing that Grain would be anxiously awaiting his arrival. Toby decided that he had better not waste any more time getting to Seaple's. So bidding the Rooter a fond farewell he mounted the little buzzer and they took their leave. As the miles and candy cotton clouds flew by, Toby reflected upon the adventures that he'd had. He hoped that the rest of his stay in this strange place was going to be just a little bit quieter than it had been up to now.

His thoughts turning to Roland, he hoped that he was alright. He still believed deep down inside that there was someone really nice trying to get out. After all he had tried to stop Raven from harming him. As he sat there pondering on all that had happened, and how his classmate had tried to help him, he was eventually stirred from his deep thoughts by Beearney who cried out. "Just around this next ridge we will be able to see the castle grounds."

Descending gently they skirted around the final mountain and into a fertile green valley beyond. Toby gasped at the beautifully presented gardens that stretched out before them with their many golden fountains shooting jets of water high into the air. Keeping a steady pace they skimmed over vast vineyards laden with purple grapes and orchards of fruit trees weighed down by heavy boughs of ripening fruit. Toby was just thinking to himself that it doesn't get any better than this when he spotted Seaple's castle in the distance. It had numerous tall white towers and colourful unfurled flags and as they got closer he suddenly felt very humble. For this was possibly the most beautiful place in the universe, he thought.

Landing in a paved courtyard, Toby slid off Beearney and gazed up at the castle. "Wow this place is just incredible" he cried as he spotted someone watching him from one of its many arch shaped windows. As he waved in greeting, whoever it was watching him, disappeared back into the shadows. Turning to Beearny he asked "did you see someone up there just now?" To his disappointment the buzzer was already sleeping soundly beside a large pink aromatic tree. Running over he tried to awaken his furry friend but after trying to arouse him unsuccessfully he left him to sleep, as he apprehensively walked up to the huge oak door alone. He knocked upon the large brass knocker nervously and waited several minutes, but no one came to answer. He rapped it again, only this time, much harder. Again no-one responding he tried the door handle and finding it unlocked, he pushed it open to reveal an enormous black and white tiled hallway. This led to a marble white staircase and an ornate balustrade.

Taking a tentative step inside, and then several more, he found himself standing at the bottom of the stairs. He waited there for several minutes but still no-one came to his numerous calls. "Hello" he yelled again hopefully. Only hearing his echo in response, as it reverberated around the smooth stone walls he decided that he'd better go and find Seaple or Grain.

Feeling alone and completely vulnerable, he started climbing up the long winding staircase. He hesitated as he sensed that someone was watching him. Looking all around, he saw that nobody else was present. So gripping the smooth marble bannister tighter, he told himself that he was just being silly and carried on up. Reaching the top of the stairs quickly he saw three long corridors which all ran off the main landing. Being unsure about which one to try first, he shouted out again. "Hello, is there anybody here?" His half-hearted call greeted only by his own mocking voice. He entered the nearest corridor and knocked the on first door. Receiving no response, he opened it and looked inside the darkened room. As his eyes slowly adjusted to the gloom, he thought that he spotted someone moving in the shadows. “Hello, is anybody in here?” He asked, wondering if it was the same person that had been watching him from the window. Suddenly, fearing whatever was lurking inside he quickly shut the door and moved to the next one. As he turned the large brass handle, two small blue furry creatures with yellow eyes and red feet ran out and started screaming in high pitched voices. Falling to his knees he tried to blot out the deafening wail, he found that he couldn’t. The noise stopping as unexpectantly as it had started. He lowered his hands as a soft feminine voice asked of him “what are you doing?”

Standing up at once, Toby spun around to see a young girl. Who was about his age and dressed all in green. Which matched her emerald coloured eyes and waist length hair. Holding out his hand in greeting, he moved forward saying “hello.”

Refusing to accept his hand, the girl laughed in response, declaring loudly “rather nosey aren’t we?”

“I was looking someone called Seaple” Toby blustered. “I didn’t mean any harm.”

“Of course you didn’t” the girl countered quickly as she pulled a velvet sash cord, setting the castles alarm bells ringing. Before Toby could explain to her why he had entered the castle uninvited, two large men appeared seemingly from nowhere and roughly picked him up by his armpits. They followed the girl as she walked purposefully along the long broad corridor. Reaching a stairwell they descended down the old smooth stone steps until they eventually reached an old wooden door. Unlocking it she cried out spitefully “throw the lying little sneak-thief in here for now. He can explain to my Father later why he was snooping around.” As requested by the haughty girl the two men threw Toby unceremoniously into the dark cell.

“Ow!” Toby cried, as he landed with a hard bump! Getting up quickly he ran back over begging for an opportunity to explain. But, ignoring him, the girl slammed the door in his face leaving him alone in the dirty cell. Sitting down against the thick wooden door, he wondered where on Earth Grain was? He mulled over the latest predicament that he found himself in. Hearing heavy breathing coming from the other side of the room, he kept as still as possible, as he listened to the irregular wheezing in the darkness. Gathering what little courage he could muster he asked warily “who’s there?”

“Who wants to know?” A harsh guttural voice rasped immediately.

“Toby Smith” he responded nervously. Receiving no reply, he added hopefully “who are you?”

The voice in the darkness replying “Flint. Not that it really matters now.”

Recognising from his anguished tone that he was suffering. Toby forgot all about his fear “are you injured?” He asked.

After a considerable time the strained voice enquired “what if I am. Are you hoping to see a shadow-man die?”

Standing up immediately, Toby edged forward in the darkness crying. “No, I don’t believe in hurting anyone or anything.”

The voice laughed sarcastically, but stopped almost immediately with a spluttering cough.

“What, someone who doesn’t hate shadow-men. What makes you so different from everyone else?”

Toby felt cold beads of sweat running down his cheek. Wiping his face with his sleeve he answered the question honestly. “As I’ve never even heard of shadow-men how can I dislike them? A stranger’s just a friend you haven’t met yet. Well at least that’s what my Mum says.”

Again there was a long silence as the shadow-man considered the answer. He spoke again, but this time it lacked sarcasm of before. “You really don’t know what a shadow-man is?”

Toby licked his dry lips, replying nervously “that’s right, I don’t.”

“Then I will tell you” the rasping voice said, “especially as I’m all but done in. A long time ago we were a proud race that held its head high, until my forefathers were tricked into giving their allegiance to a wizard called Darvock and his kin.”

“I’ve heard of him” Toby exclaimed.

“When he was killed in the Great War our vow of allegiance passed to his only daughter, the Stinger Queen. So, now we are grubbing around in her service until we, or she, dies. But, until that glorious day comes, we sneak around doing her dirty work, and that's why everybody hates us so much. Because of that and our death breath."

Toby shuffled his feet nervously which was something that he did when he was afraid. "Death breath?" He asked innocently.

Flint laughed "oh the sweet irony of it all. Here I am dying and my salvation wanders in like a fattened lamb to the slaughter."

Toby cringed, not liking the sound of that much.

The throaty voice coughed and spluttered in the dark void. "Death breath my young ignorant friend is the way that we shadow-men regain our strength when we are near to death. All we have to do is find someone healthy, like you and suck the very life out of them."

"No need for that Mr Flint" Toby shouted, taking a sea cherry from his pocket."Try this, it's worked before."

Moving forward silently, Flint was suddenly tempted by the vibrant life force that was there for the taking. Managing to resist his overwhelming urge of survival, he studied the object in Toby's hand. "What is it?" he demanded sniffing it suspiciously.

Realising that the shadow man was much closer than he thought, Toby jumped back. Determined to try and help the stranger, he bravely held out his hand once more. "It's a sea cherry, it may help."

Flint took it and swallowed it instantly. "A legendary sea cherry aye, well I'll try anything once." He whispered hoarsely as he slumped back down in the shadows and concentrated on life force.

Unable to wait, Toby asked impatiently “is it working?”Are you feeling any better?”

“Much” the shadow man responded almost instantly. “It’s incredible, and I always thought that they were just an old wife’s tale.”

Becoming a little more confident Toby walked forward. Feeling the shadow-man’s cold breath upon his face, he realised that his mysterious cell mate was up close again.

“I owe you youngster” Flint whispered gruffly as the sound of heavy footsteps appeared outside in the corridor.

Opening the door a minute later, Grain felt a rush of wind shoot past him. “What was that?” he demanded.

“A, a man called Flint” Toby stammered as he shielded his eyes from the brightly lit corridor.

“Oh no!” cried a short, bald man who was standing just behind the sandman. “Get the screamers down here quick, there’s an intruder loose in the castle.”

While security started an intensive search for the illusive Mr Flint. Grain and Seaple escorted Toby upstairs and interrogated him about what had been said in the cell. After they had heard his story, they both looked worried.

“Damn it” Seaple said sternly, “but at least that explains how the gravity machine became damaged.”

"But how did he get past the screamers and into the locked vault below?" Grain argued.

"I don't know, but does it really matter?" Seaple shouted back angrily. Calming down almost immediately he apologised. "Sorry Grain I shouldn't have snapped like that but if we can't repair the gravity machine it could mean the end of everything."

"How badly is it damaged?" Grain asked.

"Pretty bad" Seaple responded.

"And how do you feel?" Grain enquired.

Seaple moved closer, putting his arm around his old friend's shoulder. "Me, I'm okay, just a bit tired that's all."

"Are you sure?" Grain persisted. "Because you two are linked mentally aren't you."

Seaple walked over to the open window, and sitting on the broad stone ledge he smiled reassuringly. "Don't worry about me, I'm fine." Calling a waiting attendant over he asked him politely to "please fetch Drucilla."

When the girl that Toby had already had the misfortune to meet earlier entered the room moments later, Seaple yelled "are you happy now?"

Rushing over to him Drucilla asked "Father, what have I done to upset you?"

"Nothing much" he snarled. "Only locked up Grain's little friend here and allowed a shadow-man to get away after poisoning the gravity system."

The girl looked down at the floor, momentarily wilting under his gaze. Raising her head again, she answered defiantly. "But this little creep was snooping around. What was I supposed to do, just let him go?"

"No," Seaple scolded, "you should have brought him to me because I am still the custodian."

Drucilla's face softened. "But you're not well father, you need to rest."

"My health's not you're concern he shouted. But keeping out intruders is." Suddenly seeing the hurt on her face, he sighed and took her in his arms whispering softly. "I'm sorry; I didn't really mean that but everything's going wrong."

Not answering, she just buried her head deep in his chest and started crying.

Cradling her gently, Seaple comforted her.

As Drucilla left the room, Seaple declared solemnly. "I shouldn't have been so hard on her because she's had a rough time since shadow-men killed her Mother."

Toby interrupted immediately asking "are they all bad? Because Mr Flint never did me any harm did he? "

Seaple frowned and clenching his fist he stated firmly. "They're all just as bad as one another as far as I'm concerned and remember that they all work for the Stinger Queen."

Toby defended his cell-mate again, "but that isn't fair. Mr Flint said that they were all tricked into serving Darvock and his kin."

Seaple laughed sarcastically, "tricked or was he just playing another trick on you?" Anyway, forget about Flint for now because he's long gone and we have more important things to discuss. Like the great warrior that's coming from sector forty seven any day now."

"A great warrior you say" Grain asked, "any details?"

"Yes" Seaple declared smugly as he flopped down upon a large orange divan that was embroidered with gold silk. "He should be arriving any time now. As soon as he solves the little puzzle I sent to test him."

Wanting more information, Grain pressed Seaple further. "Where's he coming from this great warrior, Aluthina, Sinax, Curgoccia?"

"Earth" Seaple replied confidently. "He's from a small planet called Earth and his name is Smith, Toby Smith."

"That can't be right" Toby screamed aloud "that's me!"

Seaple's face, which had been one of confidence, quickly drained of its colour. "That's impossible" he cried, "you can't be the one that's been selected by the gravity machine to help us." He wrung his hands in desperation, "unless it's made an error due to it being damaged of course. Holding his head in his hands he groaned bitterly. "Let's pray that's not the case or we are all doomed."

Walking over to the troubled custodian Grain put his hand on his shoulder to comfort him saying "maybe old friend. But let's wait and see what tomorrow brings. Let's sleep on it tonight and discuss it further tomorrow."

"If we must" Seaple responded quietly, "If we must." With a last glance at Toby, he left the room.

"Don't worry about him" Grain Told Toby. "He'll be fine after a good nights sleep." Although he put on a brave face for Toby's benefit, Secretly, he was as worried as Seaple.

When Toby saw Seaple the next morning, he could see that he was no happier.

"Right" the custodian said, as he started the discussion about what was best to do. "It's obvious to everyone here that the gravity machine has made a serious error in bringing this young child here. Probably due to the damage caused to it by the shadow-man Flint." He stared at Toby, saying "don't worry young fella we will get you back home as soon as we can. But first we have to let the gravity machine scan your mind and make sure that you were summoned here by mistake. As it has been suggested that you could be working for the Stinger Queen." Turning quickly, he walked away crying "so follow me please." Doing as they were asked Grain walked alongside Toby, while Drucilla followed behind. They made their way down the winding stone steps which led to the lower levels, and entered an old corridor with several old wooden doors. It reminded Toby of the one that he'd been roughly carried down the night before. His thoughts returning to Flint he wondered why he had spared his life. He knew that once the sea cherry had healed his injuries he could have killed him easily, if he'd wanted to. It was what you would expect from someone who was in the service of the enemy, especially as Grain and Seaple had made it very clear that shadow-men were the scum of the Universe. He was still trying to answer these questions, when they stopped outside a large metal door.

Seaple said sternly, "what you are about to see inside here has only ever seen by custodians before but because these are troubled times. I have decided to make an exception to the rule. But I demand that you say nothing about what you see to anyone." Inserting a long brass key into the lock, he opened the huge door and led them into a cavernous room that looked like a cathedral. It had a high arched ceiling and thick weathered beams. Toby stared at the highly polished red tiles beneath their feet, glistening like giant red rubies. "Wow" he squealed in excitement "this is amazing." His jubilation was instantly curtailed, as his eyes fell on a strange silver machine that was standing in the centre of the palatial surroundings. Approximately fifty feet high, it dominated the whole area, and was covered in various dials and levers. He studied it carefully, noticing the clock on it was the one that he had repaired. "Hey, that's my Dad's clock!" he yelled.

Seaple who was not amused by his unexpected outburst, shouted angrily." Stop that racket now, this isn't a sight seeing trip. Either show some respect for the greatest piece of technology ever created, or get out. But for you're information the clock that you refer to is an integral part of the gravity system. I only sent to your planet to bring back a great warrior or wizard to help us in our time of trouble. Instead we got you, so please try to act sensibly, if you can."

Feeling rather silly, Toby took a pace back and remained quiet. Drucilla, who was standing behind him, giggled.

Seaple stared at Toby, "now that we have settled down perhaps we can conduct the test to ascertain what went wrong."

"And why we've been sent a half-pint" Drucilla quipped.

Ignoring her cutting remark, Seaple walked over to the centre of the room and sat upon a silver seat that was situated in front of the machine. Shutting his eyes, he took two long metal probes and inserted deep them into his ears. Toby could see pain etched upon his face as the long wire rods slowly disappeared. "Blessed is the machine that maintains the gravity throughout the zone" Seaple proclaimed as his bulging eyes opened wide showing countless red veins. He beckoned Toby nearer, "come and answer our questions Toby Smith" he said. "But I warn you, if you lie while giving evidence this machine will know it. So I advise you to bear that in mind and speak only the truth."

Toby gulped, suddenly realising that Seaple was deadly serious.

"State your name and age?" He demanded.

"Toby Andrew Smith, aged thirteen" Toby replied nervously.

"Place and planet of birth?" Seaple asked.

"Mend it cottage, Sniffle lane, Bristol, England." Remembering that he'd been asked also about his planet of origin. He added sheepishly, "my home is Earth."

Seaple smiled at him, as his gut feeling told him that the child before him wasn't secretly a servant of the enemy. He was just an ordinary kid, pretty much like any other that had somehow got mixed up in this mess by mistake. Realising that they had to know for certain, he put out his hands before him, saying softly. "Now touch my hands so that we can evaluate you properly."

Toby touched his outstretched palms, and was grabbed in his vice like grip. He tried to pull free as a sharp surge of electrical power shot right up his arms. "Owwwww!" He yelled as the intensity increased significantly and surged right through his body.

Seaple released him almost immediately and slumped back wearily in his seat. Recovering just enough to speak he stated "there has been no mistake. This is the right Toby Smith." Pulling up Toby's sleeve, he asked "do you have an hourglass shape on your right forearm?"

"Yes, I do" Toby answered, "It's my birthmark."

Seaple stood up and showed his arm to Grain and Drucilla. Feeling very tired, he sat back down as the two probes slowly slid back out of his head and slithered back into their allotted place upon the gravity system. Grabbing hold of Toby's shoulder for support the elderly custodian leaned upon him as he gathered all his remaining strength and shouted ceremoniously. "Let it be known here today that this Toby Smith has been verified as the person ordained to obtain the four life giving elements that are needed to restore the gravity system to full power. I call on both of you here to help him with his quest in any way that you can." He stared at Drucilla, adding "and I mean everyone, which includes you Drucilla, for if the gravity system isn't repaired soon the whole universe may be destroyed."

Taking four small glass phials from out of his purple velvet cloak he held them up saying solemnly. "These containers are to collect the four elements. The first being a pinch of the purest soil known, which is somewhere upon Glaxos minor in sector seventeen. Secondly we shall need air taken from the heart of fastest spinning tornado known which is on the inhospitable hive planet of Sting, the home of the Stinger Queen in sector eighty nine. Thirdly we shall need life giving water from the holy fountain. This is located somewhere within the arid section of the third moon that orbits the planet follies six. Finally we need fire from the only known dragon still living in the cosmos, Old Scarfle who dwells on the planet Chiacole in sector one million, nine hundred and sixty two thousand, two hundred and twenty eight." Seaple rested momentarily, before he could continue with his presentation. It was obvious that he was still in a lot of discomfort. "But remember" he said as a final word of warning. “Even if Toby manages to obtain all the four elements. He still has to incorporate them successfully into the gravity system. If not, she will implode, taking the entire zone with her.” He looked at Toby asking “any questions?”

“You gotta be joking” Toby responded “I’m only a kid! You can’t expect me to run around the universe fighting dragons and killer wasps.”

“I wish I was joking” Seaple replied, “I really do. But the gravity system has confirmed that you are the one that has been selected for this quest, and it’s too late for us to do anything about it now. Because the gravity system is breaking down a little more each day. Already several stars have deviated from their orbits and are careering dangerously through space. The sooner we get it back on line the better.”

“What happens if we do nothing, or try and fail?” Toby asked.

Seaple’s face grew grave, resting his wrinkled face upon his chubby chin he whispered soberly. “Let me try and explain our problem to you in the most simplistic terms possible. There are approximately two billion stars in your galaxy as well as ten planets that all have life, in various forms. If you multiply those by the other two millions galaxies that exist in the zone, Or the Solar System as you call it on Earth, we are talking about literally trillions of stars and thousands of planets. That’s the scale of the problem that we have. As these celestial bodies fly around the cosmos in different directions and speeds, it’s only the gravity system that makes sure that they do not detract from their orbits. It does this by constantly adjusting their gravitational pulls and realigning them when necessary."

"Are you God?" Toby asked sincerely.

Seaple laughed weakly, as he responded in a faltering voice. "No, I am not a God. Although I am well over a thousand years old. I am just a humble custodian of this wonderful piece of technology that was built by someone or something long ago." Pausing, he added "so will you undertake this grave quest to try and save the cosmos."

Panicking, Toby blurted out "but you can't really mean it. I'm, no hero."

Seaple looked at the boy before him, as he stood there trembling with his eyes and mouth wide open. "But you have been selected. What else can we do, but ask you to do as requested. So what is you're decision?"

"But it's not working properly" Toby cried. "That's the only reason it's picked me in the first place because it's flippin broken."

"That's probably true" Seaple agreed. "But we don't know for certain that it wouldn't have selected you anyway do we."

Putting his hand upon his heart Toby yelled. "Well as it seems that I've got no choice. I'll do it for my Mum and Dad, my school and the whole blinking universe!"

Seaple laughed, coughing again. He slumped back down into his seat once more.

"Father!" Screamed Drucilla as she rushed to his side, and placing his head upon her lap she whispered "Father are you all right?"

Finding it hard to speak Seaple croaked weakly. "I think that my time is running out, and that your time as the new custodian will soon begin. But promise me now, what ever happens to me that you will do all you can to help Toby." Shutting his eyes he pleaded "help him Drucilla."

Realising that he was dead, the distraught girl screamed bitterly. "This is all you're fault hero" as she left the room in tears.

Seeing that his charge was upset by Seaple's death and Drucilla's hurtful remark. Grain comforted Toby saying quietly. "Now, now young fella, don't worry. Old Grain will think of something."

After a restless night without sleep. Toby sat on the window ledge of his room thinking about his parents. Knowing that they'd be worried sick about his disappearing from his bedroom, he pictured them walking up and down in the tiny lounge. They would be trying to work out where he was, along with police. "Poor old Mum and Dad" he whispered quietly to himself. "If only I could let them know that I'm safe. But even that's not very likely now that Seaple has died."

"He's not dead," Grain the chimp answered as he entered the room and shut the door behind him. "His personal physician has said that he's only in a deep coma." He sighed adding soberly, "but he's still very weak. His only real chance to recover fully is if we can succeed in repairing the gravity system."

"That's great news" Toby cried "and just the boost that I needed. I'm really missing my parents so let's hope that we can get what we need. I still don't see what it's really got to do with me though?"

Grain sat beside him in the large arched window. "I know that you are missing your parents" he said sympathetically. "But just remember if we fail in our undertaking, they probably won't be there for you to go home to anyway."

Toby grimaced, still hoping that it was all just a dream. Pinching the back of his hand, he realised that it still was very real. "You really know how to cheer people up sandster, he said despondently as his momentary feelings of elation turned to despair.

"That maybe" Grain answered swiftly. "But let's not dwell on whether you were chosen rightly or wrongly. Let's just concentrate on the good things that we are going to make happen."

"Fair enough" Toby agreed soberly, "what happens next?"

"We meet Drucilla for breakfast" Grain responded, "and don't worry because I've had words with her and I think you will find that her attitude will be a little better this morning."

"I certainly hope so" Toby whispered as he rose and followed the sand king to meet her.

Reaching a large medieval style dining room they found Drucilla sat in front of a roaring log fire. “Morning” she said cordially, as she rose to meet them. “Come in and let’s eat” she added “because I’m absolutely starving.” Bowing graciously, she said “we can make our plans after we have filled our stomachs.”

Accepting her offer readily Grain and Toby sat down beside her upon the long wooden table which was full of every conceivable delicacy that the Solar system could provide. “Right let’s get stuck in” she purred as she picked up a huge of ribs and started munching on them veraciously.

Toby tucked his napkin into his school jersey and following suit he tried bits of just about everything that was on offer. A more conservative Grain only sipped chilled sea water. Finishing the ribs speedily Drucilla immediately moved onto the large fish that was in the middle of table. Again and again her silver knife and fork flashed as she quickly left only a bony skeleton. Not hesitating for a moment, she went straight into the enormous selection of puddings, followed several large bowls of assorted fruit.

Toby was gob smacked and cried out “wow that’s some appetite!”

Drucilla laughed as she picked up a large pitcher of water and drank it in one. After wiping her red lips she answered “I know.” Standing up she returned to the comfort zone of the crackling log fire and sat back down. “Have you given our problem any thought during night sandman?” She asked as she warmed her eight elonganated toes on the warm hearth.

Grain extended four thin legs from out of his bottom and sat down next to his host. “As a matter of fact, I have” he responded. “I have given it a great deal of thought indeed. Now it’s obvious as Seaple told us, that even if the gravity machine selected Toby in error, it’s far too late for us to do anything about it now. The only chance that we have got of being successful is if Toby tries to obtain the four sacred elements as asked. Me too, because when I found him I promised him that I’d help him get him home. To do that, I need to make sure that he succeeds, if possible.” He hesitated momentarily, and then added firmly “while you stay behind and run things from here.”

Here we go, Toby thought, that will hit a raw nerve. But he was pleasantly surprised, as Drucilla only responded quietly “yes, you’re right.” She took Grain firmly by the shoulders and stared deeply into his eyes. “I also think that you two should go as soon as possible because time is running out for my Father and the gravity system. I will kit you both out with the necessary equipment and start boosting extra power to any portals that we need to use because they are starting to fluctuate badly. Give me about an hour I’ll go and check them and get everything that you need.”

“I’m glad that you agree” Grain responded with some surprise.

“Quite,” Drucilla replied sarcastically. “But it’s only because I’m the only one that’s smart enough to operate the gravity system." She focused her gaze upon Toby, who once again felt like a little frog about to be eaten. "What about you?" she asked "is there anything that you want to ask me before you leave?"

Toby knew that there were probably a thousand things that he'd like know about but thinking quickly, he asked the one question that had been really bugging him. "Yes, there is" he responded. "When I entered beach world from the Earth and from there to here I passed through nothing more than an opening. However all the different worlds in the Solar system are separated by vast areas of space. Why didn't we need to travel in a spaceship to get to somewhere else?"

Drucilla smiled, "that's because the gravity system has the power to distort or shrink space, connecting other worlds. But, because it has been partially damaged, secret doors that are normally stable, are collapsing. That's why I need to monitor them closely and open them only when they are needed. If one malfunctions while you are both passing through it you will disintegrate."

"Like in Star Trek" Toby said.

Not knowing what Star Trek was Drucilla responded dryly "anything else?"

"Yes," he answered, "will Seaple be all right?"

"Who knows" she whispered as her attitude softened. "Let's hope so, but if you will excuse me now, I will go and fetch the equipment that you will need." Standing up, she left the room, leaving the two friends to talk.

"Golly she blows hot and cold" Toby remarked. "One minute she's friendly and the next she's as cold as ice, and can't she ever eat. It's just not natural."

The sandman smiled, "remember although she looks a lot like you she's actually a completely different species. That's why her eating habits are so different."

"She looks human" Toby cried.

"But she's not" Grain responded sternly. "Even Seaple wasn't really sure of her origin of birth when he had taken her in after her Mother had been killed." They were still discussing their mission into the unknown when Drucilla came back laden with various bits and pieces. "Right Toby" she declared, "sit down here and be prepared to feel several sharp jabs."

"W, why Toby stammered "what are you going to do to me?"

Not answering his question, Drucilla grabbed his arm and tapped it hard, until she could see a vein. "Ooh I just love this part" she cooed menacingly.

"Ow!" Toby screamed as she plunged a small needle deep into his arm. He screamed even louder as she repeated the treatment again.

"The first one is so that you can breathe properly anywhere, even underwater" she said. "While the second one will protect you from any bacteria that you come into contact with. Finally" she laughed, "there is this. A neural lobe communicator which will enable you to understand and communicate with any species that you meet."

Toby stared at the evil looking device in her hands. “No way” he screamed. But before he could do his usual trick of running away. Grain grabbed hold of him tight. “Now, now young man, where do you think that you’re going?” He asked, as his booming laugh filled the room.

“Let me go!” Toby shouted angrily as the seemingly deaf sandman held on tight to his struggling prisoner.

While a grinning Drucilla teased “come on hero. Just one more jab and it’ll be all over.” Moving forward menacingly she held out the horrible looking object in both hands making sure that her patient could see the long needle attached.

“No!” Toby screamed as he felt suddenly ill and fainted.

Chapter Four
The Ogre's Garden

Toby opened his eyes and looked up into the face of Grain who said cheerfully "come on it's nearly time for us to leave."

Toby rubbed his aching head with his hands. "Okay, but only as long as that blimming great big needle thing's gone."

Grain winked, replying "all done."

Standing, Toby felt dizzy. Taking the Sandman's arm for support he mumbled "I feel kind of woozy."

"I'm not surprised" Grain responded "especially as Drucilla gave you several more inoculations while you were knocked out. She said that you can't be too careful when visiting other worlds with hostile environments and dangerous bugs."

"I suppose she's right" Toby agreed as he sat back down.

He was still taking deep breaths when Drucilla walked in with a cheeky grin on her face, "don't worry" she chuckled "you should be feeling much better soon. Then you two can go and zip around the zone while I sit here twiddling my thumbs." Sitting next to Toby she added "its okay I'm only kidding really, I realise that someone intelligent has to do all the technical stuff. Now listen carefully to what I am going to tell you because it's very important. All the jabs that you have had will enable you to breath properly on the other worlds that you visit but they will only last for about a week. You need to finish your task and get back here in that time or else!"

Toby visibly winced as the frightening thought of suffocation came into his mind.

Not noticing his discomfort Drucilla carried on talking, "yeah, well that's about it really except that you need to wear this bracelet." Thrusting a silver armlet upon his wrist she added " keep it on at all times and don't lose it, this is how I'm gonna track you as you move from one place to another. Once you have collected an element press this red button and it will tell me that you have been successful and I'll open the portal into your next destination. After you have collected all four elements, press this green button and I'll bring you straight back here."

"Right" Toby said as he tried to psyche himself up, although deep down he wondered if his courage would hold up as it wasn't really his strong suit.

Bravado and testosterone taking over he stood up crying “come on Grain, let’s go and get em.”

“That’s the spirit” Grain agreed, picking up the small leather case that contained the four glass collection phials.

“Remember” Drucilla stated sombrely “you only need a minute pinch of each element its quality, not quantity that counts.” Standing up she pulled Toby onto his feet and embracing him she whispered quietly “sorry about yesterday and I really mean that, take good care of yourself and watch out for stingers.”

Toby smiled and wondered if she had ever been teased about having bright green hair. But, just as he was about to ask her she pressed a button on her own ring and bustled them into the open doorway.

“Flaming heck!” Toby yelled in surprise as they dropped out of thin air and landed upon a giant rotten mushroom. “The scheming little minx I bet she did that on purpose.”

“Probably “ Grain laughed “but I think that she likes you really.”

“She’s got a strange way of showing it” Toby responded brushing the smelly pink mushroom flesh from his shorts. Remembering the friendly buzzer he mumbled sadly “darn it I never said goodbye to Barney.”

“Don’t worry about that too much” the sandman answered “from my limited experience of buzzers he’ll find you if he wants to. They have a sort of sixth sense which can lock on to anyone that they have bonded with and..." His voice trailed off as he noticed that all the grass and trees around them was either dead or dying.

Bending down Toby picked up a handful of dry soil saying "this can't be what we're looking for because it's little more than dust."

Grain laughed, "did you really think that finding purest elements in the entire zone would be that easy. Just shoot out and pick them up and get back home in time for tea. I don't think so" he added sarcastically.

"So where shall we look?" Toby asked.

Gesturing that he didn't really know which direction to take Grain the chimp suggested "let's just walk for now and see where it leads us."

"Okay" Toby agreed "that good enough for me." Walking along the narrow dirt track leaving a thick cloud of dust billowing behind them they wondered why this world was so arid. The atmosphere not really seeming that hot or dry.

After they had been following the dirt track for a few miles Grain asked Toby "have you noticed that there are no birds singing or insects? I think that's because every living creature has either died or left this place because it's so inhospitable. It looks as if every last drop of moisture has been sucked right out of the place, but it's not like a desert where it's happened over thousands of years. Whatever catastrophe occurred here has happened recently otherwise all these dying plants wouldn't still be here, they'd have rotted off and returned to the soil long ago."

"We all know who's responsible for this terrible mess" a squeaky little voice behind them said angrily. Turning around they saw a strange little man who was sat against the withered husk of a dying tree. "It's a crying shame" he moaned bitterly "because this forest and the valley used to be green and the giant mushrooms that grew here were plentiful and really tasty due to the fresh mountain spring water that ran down into the valley from up North. It's all dried up now like everything else around here because that selfish Ogre altered the course of the river."

"Ogre" Grain asked, "what ogre?"

"The one that dammed the river of course. But nobody was able to do anything about it so they all moved into the next valley before he ate them."

"A, ate them!" Toby stammered nervously as his old habit of shuffling his feet returned.

"Yes, ate them" the little man confirmed. "He'll squish just about anybody and eat them for his dinner."

"Are you sure he does that kind of thing?" Grain asked looking concerned.

"Am I sure? Am I sure? Of course I'm sure" the man yelled angrily. "Because I've heard them screaming as he squished them with his masher."

Toby hoped that Grain wasn't going to ask what the ogre's masher was, but of course he did.

"What's a masher?" Grain enquired as Toby cringed and shut his eyes.

Pulling upon his long white whiskers the odd little man responded “it’s a big wooden club that he squishes you with before he bakes you in a pie. But I can’t stand here gossiping all day I’m off and join the others.” Scratching his chin he added sadly “they only left because it wasn’t worth staying here any longer. What with no mushrooms and everything drying up and people getting squished all the time.”

“You’re certain that it’s this ogre that squishes people?” Grain asked.

“Of course I am” the man responded. “How can you miss a great big ogre like that whose always covered in compost.”

“What do you mean, compost?” Grain asked curiously.

The stranger sighed “questions, questions and even more blooming questions. It’s said that he loves gardening and that he produces the purest compost ever made because of a secret ingredient, which I think may be the brain juice of people that he’s squished.”

“That’s very interesting “Grain said, fingering one of the little glass phials in his small leather pouch.”Well thank you for all your help” he said “but we had better be going now to see if this ogre will give us some of his soil.”

“You can’t be serious” the man said “he’ll squish you and extract your brain juices.”

“That’s as maybe” Grain replied sheepishly “but we have no choice in the matter because we desperately need some of his compost, especially if it's as pure as you claim." Grain hesitated, and then asked hopefully "I don't suppose that you would you like to show us where he lives?"

"You must be joking" the man cried becoming very agitated. "It's a stupid idea to go up there in the first place but if you two want to go and get yourselves squished, leave me out of it."

Replying "thanks" sarcastically Grain walked briskly away, leaving Toby struggling to keep up.

"Slow down" Toby pleaded as he ran alongside the animated sandman "it's no good if we just go rushing in."

Slowing down almost immediately Grain kept a more reasonable pace so that Toby could keep up.

Taking his hand Toby said "don't let's worry about it now, we'll think of something when we get there."

Following the narrow path along the decimated countryside they walked along in single file until the dirt track became much wider and started getting steeper. Realising that this was probably the hill that led up to the ogre's dwelling place they spoke in whispers, as fear suddenly took a hold of both of them "Not long now" Toby mouthed silently as they started rounding a sharp corner.

"I suppose so" Grain replied becoming fearful that he'd never see beach world again. He gripped Toby's hand tighter as they crept slowly towards the unknown. Suddenly stopping, Grain pulled Toby into cover behind some old twisted roots.

"Wait" he whispered cautiously "there's a building up ahead."

"I see it" Toby answered "it's massive."

Grain gulped responding hoarsely "whoever lives in there must be pretty big, so let's try to be quiet."

Toby smiled weakly as his knees started knocking and teeth started chattering. It reminded him of the time when he and Roland had been sat outside the headmistress's office. Trying to put a brave face on it he replied quietly "I'm ready when you are."

"Right" Grain agreed in hushed tones.

Toby waited for the sandman to start creeping forward, but after a few minutes he still hadn't moved. Realising that something was wrong he nudged him and waited for a response, but it never came. He elbowed him again, but once more he received no answer to his urging. "Grain" he said softly "what's up why aren't we moving?"

Grain looked away in shame "I can't move" he said "I'm terrified and my legs feel like lead."

Toby couldn't believe that Grain, a former war veteran had frozen. Gripping his long sandy fingers gently he said "it's probably better if only one of us goes anyway; watch my back while I take a quick peek and come back as quick as I can."

"Are you sure?" Grain whimpered as Toby crept slowly past him.

"I'm sure" Toby answered as he crawled off quietly on his hands and knees trying to keep under cover. As he neared the building he found that he was becoming more exposed. Although the front door was still about fifty metres away. He looked at the huge barred windows which had matching floral pink curtains, but couldn't see any sign of life. He knew that he couldn't get any closer without breaking cover completely and realised that it was still several hours until darkness fell. Acting impulsively in the true Smith family tradition he jumped up and ran toward the house as fast as he could. Intending to have a quick look inside a window and report back to the waiting sandman. Reaching what he believed was the safety of the porch he stood against the wall for cover. The front door suddenly opening with a loud creak a deep voice growled "ooh how lovely a visitor."

Toby stared at the twelve dirty yellow toenails that were sticking out of an old pair of broken leather sandals. Reluctantly he raised his head to see who owned such a huge pair of big smelly feet. His eyes bulged out of his head as two hairy legs that were the size of two tree trunks supported an enormous pot belly that was overhanging a thick leather belt. His legs start shaking as he forced his eyes upward past two muscular hairy arms and a thick wrinkled bull neck. His mouth dropped open, as he stared in disbelief at the ogre's bowling ball face which had sparkling baby blue eyes and only three teeth.

"H, hello" he answered timidly spotting the ogre's untidy crop of bright red hair. Survival instincts kicking in immediately his first thought was too run away, although he knew that with his massive stride the enormous ogre would probably catch him easily. Deciding that his only chance was to try and play it cool he answered stupidly “I was passing and thought that I’d pop in for a chat.”

“Good” the smiling giant responded, opening the door a little more. “You had better come in then unless you are going to run away like everyone else. It’s been so long since I had a visitor, don’t folk realise that it’s just plain rude to do that, especially when I have something simmering upon the stove.”

“The stove” Toby whispered hoarsely as his throat suddenly dried up.

The ogre bent down and looked right into his face asking “are you sure that you’re not thinking of running away?”

“N, no, I’m not” Toby stammered, realising that he couldn’t run anyway as his legs were numb with fear.

The ogre grinned with his nearly toothless grin “in that case you had better come in for some tea; by the way I’m Bradollbecknat.”

“Great” Toby whimpered sarcastically as he stepped inside the brightly lit room and heard the door shut firmly behind him. Scanning the room for a way to escape he saw that all the walls were made of thick stone while the windows were high and fastened with heavy locks. Well and truly caught he studied the ogre’s meagre collection of furniture which consisted of three huge wooden stools which were nearly as tall as he was. Seeing a large old rack that held a large grey club, he knew that it had to be the dreaded masher he'd been told about. His face dropped as he spotted the large open fire at the other end of the room and a big black cooking pot that was hissing noisily. His eyes followed the trail of the hot steam as it enveloped the long line of shiny cooking utensils hanging upon the wall. It's the kitchen he thought, I'm in his kitchen.

His host walked over and leant down upon the tall stone mantle piece making Toby realise just how big he really was. At least sixteen feet tall he thought, as he considered how much someone that big ate.

"Sit down and let's chat" the ogre said warmly "because I don't get that many visitors."

I'm not surprised if you keep eating them Toby thought, as he answered nervously "that's a pity."

"Yes it is" the ogre responded sadly "do you think it's because of my unusual eating habits?"

Toby who had just managed to climb upon the high stool, nearly fall off again. "I don't know" he answered as he started trembling more than ever.

"Because some folk think that we vegetarian ogre's are being a bit strange."

"They do?" Toby replied quietly suddenly realising what his host had said, he asked "sorry can you repeat that."

"Why, are you hard of hearing?" the ogre asked looking rather concerned. Leaning closer he shouted "I said that some folk think that we vegetarians are a bit odd."

Toby was flabbergasted by the unexpected revelation.

Bradollbecknat, who was still waiting for an answer yelled noisily “hello, can you hear me?”

Feeling just a little more confident about his chances of not being squished and eaten Toby asked “you don’t eat meat?”

His host giggled childishly “nope, I haven’t eat anything other than fruit and vedge for over forty years, why do you ask?”

Toby could feel his face flush red as he answered sheepishly “I thought that ogre’s ate meat.”

“Not since I lost nearly all me teeth in an accident “Bradollbecknat responded with a broad smile.

“I’m jolly glad to hear it” Toby said feeling relieved.

Catching on the ogre howled with delight “ha, ha, I bet you thought that I was going to eat you, didn’t you? Go on, admit it.”

“It had crossed my mind” Toby answered honestly relaxing a little more although he still had the nagging doubt about whether the ogre’s claim was really true or not because of what the man at the bottom of the hill had said. Knowing that any chance of escape was still unlikely, he took a deep breath and asked “I heard that anyone coming here would be squished and eaten.” He waited anxiously hoping that the huge creature wouldn’t take offence.

“Why would anybody tell you that?” the giant demanded angrily.

Seeing that he'd opened up a can of worms and saying the first thing that came into his head Toby answered stupidly "maybe it's because of all the terrible screams that they hear."

"Screams, what screams?" the ogre shouted. "Fruit and veg don't scream when they're being cooked do they?"

"No, not that I'm aware of" Toby quickly reassured him.

"Who is it that has been spreading all these malicious rumours?" Bradollbecknat yelled picking up his heavy masher from the nearby rack.

Toby slipped down off the stool intending to run again, but hesitated as the ogre suddenly bent over and started touching his toes and taking deep breaths. "Calm down and breath deeply" he whispered as he shut his eyes and tried to relax. Opening them again several minutes later he laughed aloud and declared "its okay, its okay I've calmed down. In the past I would have squished you for saying something like that, although it was true. But I really don't do that sorta stuff anymore unless someone tries to steal my compost."

Toby bit his lip, "you really don't eat meat any more?"

"Not a morsel" his host responded seriously "hand on heart and hope to die, bite my nose if I tell a lie."

Toby climbed back upon the tall stool as his smiling host put his massive weapon back into the rack. Sitting back down he said apologetically "I'm sorry that I lost my temper there for a moment, just occasionally my nasty old character resurfaces and I get the desire to squish someone. Although I can tell you honestly, I wouldn't eat them even if I did squish them. You just can't beat a good old rhubarb tart with creamy custard or fresh corn on the cob with lots of hot butter and a plate full of chips. Oh, did I tell you that I make my own bread as well" he added, beaming with pride. "But whenever I talk about food it makes me hungry so you just sit there and I'll see what I can find for us to eat in the larder." Standing up awkwardly he squeezed his huge bulk into the walk in cupboard at the end of the kitchen. Toby was still wondering whether the ogre was really a vegetarian or someone that enjoyed playing with his food before eating it. Deciding to keep his wits about him until he knew for sure he waited patiently until his host returned carrying several large platters. "Here we are" he said happily as he put several dishes of food upon the wooden table. "I'm afraid that we will have to make do with what we've got because I wasn't expecting a guest. If I had known that you were coming I would have cooked something special. Never mind, it's too late to worry about that now."

Toby watched the happy ogre as he laid out his impromptu feast. But, remembering how quickly he had turned angry before, he knew that he had to be careful about what he said in future. So being diplomatic he said "this meal looks absolutely wonderful."

"That's awfully nice of you to say so" his host responded, arranging the various dishes until they were just where he wanted them. Standing back he surveyed his labour of love "hm, not really perfect" he said "but it will have to do." Satisfied with his arrangement of the food he sat back down and poured out two steaming hot drinks. One in a small mug that was big enough for his tiny guest, and another that resembled a small bath tub. Placing the smaller drinking vessel in front of Toby he picked up his beverage and started drinking it greedily. Toby watched in awe as he emptied the large container in one long sip. Wiping his lips upon his hairy thick arm the ogre watched his guest closely.

Although he was a little apprehensive about what was actually in the drink Toby decided that he had better try it in case he set his host off again. He sipped the smooth liquid cautiously, but too his surprise he found that it tasted really good. Taking a deep breath he drank the rest in one go, "wow" he said as he placed his empty container back upon the table "that's incredible, what's in it?"

Smiling from ear to ear the ogre rubbed his hands together. "I was hoping that you'd like it because that's my favourite drink. It's made from my own ear wax, plus various nuts and lots of fresh fruit."

Toby now wished that he'd hadn't asked what was in the concoction. Making sure that his feeling of revulsion about drinking ear wax stayed hidden, he sampled the rest of the food that was on offer. It included a variety of home made fruit and vegetable dishes served on something that looked a bit like a Yorkshire pudding. Knowing that it was probably better not to know what all the ingredients were, he ate as much as he could to impress his contented host. Forcing down a last mouthful of fruit pie, he reluctantly drank a second cup of ear wax and settled down next to Bradollbecknat beside the roaring fire.

His host warmed his feet as he nattered on happily about his youth and his beloved garden.

"Yeah," he began somewhat ashamedly "I admit it; I did eat anybody and everything that I could catch when I was younger because I didn't know any better. But, after I had an accident and lost nearly all my teeth I found that I couldn't chew properly any more, eating loads of green stuff I found that it could be just as tasty as meat, so I stopped eating meat all together. That was when I built this house to live in and started creating my lovely garden. It was really hard work at first as I diverted the course of the river to provide fresh water and built a big wall to keep out any trespassers. I persevered though as I knew that I had to protect the very special compost that I was making." A big grin appearing on his face the ogre added smugly "which just happens to be the best in the entire zone." His expression of pride suddenly changed to a frown he rubbed his eyes adding sadly "but it's so very lonely with no-one but my singing fleas for company."

"What are singing fleas?" Toby asked.

"Here they are" the ogre answered proudly "these are my little babies." Stretching over, he pulled a dirty old cloth from off a rickety old wooden cage and he shook it vigorously. "Come on you sleepy little devils wake up and sing for Daddy."

Toby stared in amazement as three large pink prawn like creatures slowly stirred. Although his fascination soon turned to one of horror as they all started screaming loudly in a high pitched wail which reminded him of the hideous noise that had been created by the screamers back at Seaple's castle. Looking over at his host he saw that his eyes were shut and he was smiling, which was just how his Dad looked when he relaxed listening to beloved jazz. It dawned upon him that the contented ogre was actually enjoying the awful experience. Gritting his teeth he refrained from putting his fingers in his ears until they stopped.

Covering his pets up once more the ogre smiled saying "there, there, go back to sleep now and I'll feed you some boiled cabbage later." Turning back to Toby he asked "have you ever heard anything like that before?"

"No" Toby replied "I can honestly say that I haven't." Before Bradollbecknat could answer him there was a loud knock at the door. Rising to answer it at once the ogre said in a surprised tone "now who can that be?"

Opening the door he looked down to see an angry looking sandman who yelled instantly "get my friend out of your oven now or you're for it."

"Grain" Toby shouted quickly "don't worry, I'm all right it's the singing fleas that are making all the noise."

“Well that’s okay” Grain answered thankfully, suddenly realising just how big the giant figure before him was.

“Well don’t just stand there” the excited ogre cried “come on in and let’s get to know each other.”

Quickly changing his oversized fists back into normal sized hands the Grainster nervously squeezed past the barrel chested giant to join his little chum by the fire. “Are you sure that you’re okay?” he whispered nervously.

Taking the sandman in his arms Toby said “yeah I’m fine. Now let me introduce you properly to our wonderful host Bradollbecknat.”

After the introductions were concluded and Grain was satisfied in his own mind that they were reasonably safe he listened intently as Toby told the ogre about what was going on in the zone and asked him if they could have a pinch of soil from his garden to fulfil the first part of their quest.

Shaking his head solemnly Bradollbecknat said “no because each and every grain is precious to me.”

Toby was disappointed by the negative response but responding in the never say die Smith family tradition he immediately started trying to find a solution to the problem that faced him while Bradollbecknat and the sandman chatted together. Suddenly jumping up Toby shouted enthusiastically “I think I’ve got it!” Walking towards the back door he said “come on Brad show us your garden.”

Standing up instantly their host could hardly contain his excitement as he led them outdoors into his patch of paradise. Toby and the sandman rocked back on their heels in amazement as they studied the numerous scented flowers, fruit laden trees and many vegetables that covered several acres. At first they strolled at a leisurely pace around the vast property discussing the plants that were growing there. But, constantly urged on by the impatient ogre they ended up nearly running as he proudly showed off his labour of love to outsiders for the first time. “Over here” he yelled anxiously “come and see my lovely dwarf fruit trees. I’ve seventy six different sorts from several worlds you know.” But before they could really see them properly, the ogre’s excitement getting the better of him he would rush them off to see something else. Toby noticed that although the river fed several large water wheels and fountains most of the water was diverted through a large pipe back out of the garden into a different direction from its original course. Toby watched the beaming ogre, who was as excited as a kid with a new toy. But, no matter how hard he tried to slow him down he couldn’t as he kept on at a considerable pace until they had seen everything but his secret compost heap. Sitting Bradollbecknat down on a large flat boulder Toby told him honestly “this is without doubt a garden of great beauty and you must be very proud of it.”

“Yep, I am” the beaming ogre confessed.

"Good" Toby agreed "because you should be proud. To achieve all this on your own is an absolute miracle, but are you going to show us everything, as I would really like to see your compost heap that you claim is the best in the whole zone. After I see it, if we agree with your findings I may have an interesting offer to put to you."

Becoming quiet Bradollbecknat sat thinking for a while. Eventually, after a lot of head scratching he said "I will show you my compost heap because I like you. If you both promise not to try and steal any. If you try I won't be happy."

Toby could see by the ogre's stony face that he wasn't kidding but hoping that he had found a way to compromise, he answered instantly "we agree."

Hesitating momentarily, the ogre again seemed uncertain about whether to comply with their request or not. But, after yet another long pause to reflect upon their request he pulled hard upon an old rope revealing a hidden part of the garden. "Here you are" he said suspiciously "see it if you must but just remember the promise that you made because if I find as much as a single grain missing I will know whose responsible."

They followed the ogre into a secluded area that had been cleverly hidden from view by a complicated series of ropes and weights. Toby suddenly smelt a wonderful intoxicating fragrance that filled the warm air with its heady sweet perfume. Moving closer it became stronger until it was nearly overpowering. "Wow!" he yelled excitedly. "What a lovely smell, is that the compost."

"It is" Braddollbecknat confirmed "the finest in the entire zone."

"Can I touch it?" Toby asked.

"Okay" the giant figure responded "but remember what happens to anyone that tries to steal any."

"I haven't forgotten the masher or that I've given you my word" Toby purred as he stuck his hand straight into the dark welcoming earth and felt it crumble between his fingers. This is really great stuff" he said as he let the much needed soil fall back into the black large pile. Turning back to the ogre he said "you are right this has to be the purest compost ever made."

"That's because of the sugar bee nest underneath it" the proud ogre confided, feeling just a little bit happier now that his guest had returned his beloved compost back to where it belonged.

"But" Toby continued "I want to show you another garden close by."

"Oh goody" Bradollbecknat yelled with excitement "is it very far?"

"No, not far" Toby replied as he led the way back indoors "open the front door and I'll take you there now."

Grain who was following close behind wondered just what in tar nation Toby was up to as he guided the anxious ogre back down the dirt track. When they were about a mile from his house Toby stopped asking the ogre "what do you think of this garden?"

"Garden" Bradollbecknat replied looking extremely puzzled "this looks more like a piece of old wasteland."

"By changing the direction of the river" Toby said "you have single handily nearly destroyed this forest and valley, forcing all the creatures who lived there to move away.

Grain cringed expecting a giant hairy fist to come down and flatten them both. But he was pleasantly surprised when the shocked ogre reacted tearfully "how could I know that I caused this to happen I haven't been out of the house for years."

"True" Toby countered quickly "but accidental or not you are still responsible. So what do you intend to do about it?"

"What I can I do?" the distraught ogre wailed sadly, holding his head in his large hairy hands.

"You can do the decent thing and repair the mess that you have caused" Toby answered softly as he put his tiny hand upon the bawling ogre's knobbly knee.

"How can I do that?" He asked between tears.

"By making the ultimate sacrifice" Toby whispered. "By unblocking the dam so that most of the water flows back into the valley where it belongs. You waste most of it anyway by diverting it out through the back of your garden. Why not let it run where nature intended it to. Then if you sprinkle your magical compost onto this barren place you can help return it back to its former glory. As a gardener you must see that it's only right that you must atone for your terrible mistake."

Wiping away his tears the distraught ogre sat thinking about Toby's words and deciding that he was right he asked quietly "if I restore the water back to the valley surely that will be enough to make it grow again without using my compost."

"I don't believe that it will" Toby argued "because this barren land needs all the help that it can get if it is ever to recover properly. Your compost is necessary to give it that all important boost, it can be the difference between success and failure."

"It's taken me forty years to make it" the ogre yelled as tears started welling up in his eyes once more."

Toby climbed up onto his broad thigh and stared right into his crystal blue eyes saying "I know that you love it as most creatures love their children but if you do this good deed not only will you feel much better it will be like you are extending you're garden. You could make this arid scrubland green again."

"On my own, it'll take me a hundred years at least" the ogre cried.

"Oh no it won't" Toby replied quickly "not if friends help you."

"But I don't have any friends" Bradollbecknat moaned sadly as he burst out crying again.

"Look Brad" Toby said "would having friends be more important to you than keeping your compost?"

Stopping crying immediately the friendly giant answered "of course it would Id love to have friends visit me and a vegetarian ogress to cook for."

"Well there's our answer" Toby suggested "if you divert all of the water that you don't need back into the river bed and help regenerate the valley with your compost. In return I will get the people who lived in the wood to return and visit you as often as possible. Then, I shall find you a beautiful ogress."

"Really?" Bradollbecknat yelled.

"Really" Toby promised.

"Yippee! the ogre shouted aloud as he put Toby back down upon the ground and ran back up the hill yelling "not gonna be lonely any more."

"That seems to have worked out okay" Grain whispered sarcastically, "but will the forest people come back and visit him?" Oh, and by the way where are we going to find a vegetarian ogress?"

"One thing at a time" Toby answered "forget about the ogress for now. Let's just go and sort out the forest people first." Leading the sandman back down the hill Toby saw that the old man was still sat by the tree, "still here?" he asked curiously.

"I waited to see if you got squished" the man answered. "How did you escape?"

"We never escaped" Grain responded "the ogre let us come down here to find you"

"Why?" the man asked looking worried.

"Because he's lonely" Grain answered quickly "he wants you and the other wood folk to visit him."

"What so he can eat us?" the man shouted angrily.

"He's a vegetarian" Toby responded.

"How can he be?" the man demanded. "He's an ogre and they all eat meat."

"Not this one" Toby assured him, "and as a gesture of good faith he's going to let the river flow down into the valley again. He's also going to spread his special compost around the valley and wood to help generate new growth."

"And he won't eat us?" the man asked again.

"Definitely not" they both said together.

Sitting down the old man thought about what he been told. Taking a deep breath he said "well if the river starts flowing again and he helps bring everything back to life I'll go into the next valley and bring the others back. They didn't really want to leave anyway, it just became impossible for them to stay here any longer."

Hearing the sound of rushing water Toby ran over to the dried up river bed just as a wall of white water came speeding down from the hill side "there you are" he shouted "just as Bradollbecknat promised."

The old man nodded in agreement, but stopped as he felt the earth suddenly shaking beneath his feet "what's that?" he asked apprehensively.

"It's only me" the ogre shouted happily in answer as he suddenly appeared pushing a large wooden wheelbarrow full of black compost. Stopping quickly he thrust out his huge hand to the old man crying "hello I'm your neighbour from up the hill and I believe that I have caused you and your companions great suffering. I would just like to say that I'm sorry and will do whatever I can.

Please accept this first barrow of my compost as an apology and get ready for a zillion more."

Taking one step back and then two forward the man shook the ogre's enormous hand saying "that's very nice of you, very nice indeed. It makes me feel rather ashamed because if we had taken the trouble to make your acquaintance and tell you what was happening down here instead of just assuming the worst the forest and valley wouldn't be in the state that it's in now."

Interrupting him immediately Toby said "forget the past and let's just look to the future." Taking command of the situation he added "Brad you keep those barrow loads of compost coming while our friend here goes to bring back all the forest people to help. Once we've moved every last barrow load I think that we should have a party up at your place so that everybody can get to know each other."

"Great idea" Bradollbecknat shouted as he jumped up and down with excitement spilling most of the compost in the process. "I'll go straight back up and get some more now." Tipping up the remaining contents of his load he ran back up the hill shouting "gonna cook for a party."

As he disappeared from view still singing at the top of his voice the old man laughed "all right I'm convinced I'll go and tell the others that it's okay to come back. I shouldn't be that long, perhaps a few hours or so.

"Great" Toby replied "now all we have got to do is to try and find a vegetarian ogress."

"Why didn't you say so" the man said "there's one who lives all alone in the valley where my friends are. She's the main reason why they moved there because she's friendly and doesn't eat meat."

"Brilliant" Toby yelled seeing a distinct possibility of a happy ending. "See if she will come to the party and tell her that there's a particularly good looking bachelor ogre who's single and loves to cook."

"I will" the man answered as he hurried away.

Going back up the hill they saw Bradollbecknat running back down with another barrow load of compost.

"Can't stop to talk now" he cried "I'm too busy what with all this compost to move and a load of baking to do."

"You'll have to stop soon" Toby yelled "because you may be getting a very special guest later."

Stopping in his tracks Bradollbecknat shouted "ooh lovely, I just love surprises."

Several hours later, after he had reluctantly taken a bath and had his hair brushed the excited ogre ran over to see who was knocking at the front door and nearly fainted when he saw a huge crowd of forest folk with the prettiest ogress that he'd ever seen. "Please come in" he squealed with delight as he immediately made a beeline for her. "Hello" he said politely as gently took her by the hand and led her inside.

The morning after the party Grain and Toby awoke to see all the partied out forest people sleeping virtually everywhere. Creeping outside quietly they about strolled in the early sunlight. Grain took Toby by the arm saying “now that our promise had been kept to the big fellow we should really be moving on to find the second element.”

“I agree but not without saying goodbye first” Toby answered sadly. Leaving the sandman soaking up the energy giving rays of sunlight. He ran back into the house to bid his friend Bradollbecknat farewell. Unable to find him anywhere inside, he went out into the garden and found him asleep with the snoring ogress. Watching them lying together in each others arms Toby decided not to disturb him after all. But as he tried to tiptoe quietly away he heard him whisper gratefully “thank you Toby.”

Turning around Toby bowed graciously saying “I can assure you that the pleasure was all mine. Be happy and if I’m ever this way again I’ll call in on you.”

“You’d better” the sleepy ogre whispered as he shut his eyes and snuggled in closer.

Shutting the front door Toby walked over to the sandman saying “let’s grab a pinch of soil and see where that little minx sends us off to next.”

Chapter Five
The Stinger Queen

Pressing the green button on his wristband. Toby waited until the portal into the next world opened. Entering the doorway he and Grain clambered out the other side into a very different type of world. "Crikey!" he shouted as he surveyed the harsh and foreboding landscape. "This doesn't look very nice at all."

Grain remained silent.

"Did you hear me?" Toby asked as he watched several sinister black tornados whizzing by on the distant horizon.

"I heard you" Grain responded. "But it's dangerous here."

Toby took the worried sandman by the arm. "You knew that we had to come."

"I know, but stingers will be patrolling their territory" he mumbled.

"But we need the purest air possible" Toby argued "and that's here."

Grain's face dropping, he said softly. "I know but if she catches us she will suck you dry as a bone." He hesitated as he pondered upon the meaning of his own terrifying words. "Not a very nice prospect is it, especially as we have to try and get inside a tornado as well."

"Inside" Toby asked immediately. "How can we do that with it moving around all the time?"

"That's the problem" Grain agreed. "That and whether I freeze again."

"Now look here buddy" Toby replied. "Without you I wouldn't have even got this far. As for being frightened, I'm shaking in my shoes as well but we can get through this as long as we stick together. So, let's try and figure out how we are going to get inside a tornado. Remember whatever happens there's nobody I would rather be with than you."

"You really mean that? Grain asked.

"Of course I do" Toby assured him looking over his shoulder at the hostile world that confronted them. As if it had heard his inner most thoughts, a distant volcano exploded filling the air with boiling hot lava and suffocating ash. It suddenly dawned upon the frightened child that this task was going to be much harder than the last.

"It looks pretty grim though doesn't it" Grain mumbled as they descended precariously down the rough mountain track into the scarred valley below.

"It does" Toby agreed, "but at least this time Drucilla never dropped us onto a mouldy old mushroom."

They trudged down the dry and dusty slope. Toby's throat ached and he thought that his lungs were going to burst as the hot stifling air and poisonous gases made it difficult to breathe.

"It's a good job that you had all those shots or you'd be a gonner by now" Grain yelled.

Toby nodded silently in agreement as he concentrated on negotiating the rubble strewn ledge that meandered meaninglessly in this direction, then that. But, as time passed they just didn't seem to be getting anywhere. Stopping, Toby shouted "this is taking us forever."

"I know" Grain yelled back miserably. "But there's nothing that we can do about it is there?"

"I don't know about that" Toby called back as a mischievous twinkle came into his eye. "If you changed into a sled, I could ride you down."

"It's far too steep and rough for that" Grain whimpered unhappily.

"Grain," Toby said in a firm authoritative manner. "Come on, you know that it makes sense."

"I suppose so" the disgruntled sandman agreed, slipping reluctantly into the form of a flat disc that had two handles and a rather bumpy looking seat.

"Can you make this seat better?" Toby moaned as he climbed aboard and tried to get comfortable.

"If you don't like it, we can always switch places and I'll ride you." The sandster quickly retorted.

"No this is fine" Toby responded as he finally settled and stopped squirming around. Sliding slowly down the mountainside at first, they soon picked up momentum and accelerated quickly as they sped rapidly towards the bottom. Again and again Toby thought they were going to tip up as they hit every bump and hole that was there. Eventually, as much by luck as anything else, they reached the dusty valley floor safely. As they finally slowed to a grinding halt, Toby jumped out and sighed thankfully.

"What was that little groan for? Grain asked.

"Well that ride was a little hairy at times" Toby responded.

"How can you say such a thing" Grain countered. "I was in complete control at all times."

"You could have fooled me" Toby laughed. "Especially when we nearly tipped up."

"Nearly tipped up, when?" Grain asked incredulously.

"Oh forget it, Toby teased. "Let's just be grateful we made it down in one piece."

"Now you just wait a minute you little..." Grain shouted. But seeing the wicked glint in his friend's eye, he realised that Toby was just pulling his leg. Tutting aloud, he added sarcastically "which way shall we walk, or do you want to ride again?" "It doesn't really matter which way we go does it because we shall never be able to get inside a twister. Unless it decides to stop and pick us up that is."

"Maybe not" Toby shouted, as he tried to make himself heard above the rising wind. "But we have got to manage it somehow, everybody's depending on us."

Grain winced knowing that the stakes were high, too high. Knowing that they never had another choice he headed off towards the distant purple mountains that were being relentlessly pummelled by sheets of driving rain and several ominous dark funnels of angry twisters.

Watching the two travellers struggle against the violent forces of nature in her looking glass, the stinger Queen laughed malevolently as she drank fresh blood from her ornately carved golden goblet. Becoming bored watching her puny adversaries, she left her mirror to interrogate Raven and his trembling wife. "Are those two pathetic creatures the ones that have caused you so much trouble?"

"Yes" Raven answered timidly, bowing before his Queen who was waiting impatiently for answers. "Yes, that is the Earth child Toby Smith and the sandman they call Grain."

"My Father's murderer, but he doesn't look very dangerous "she remarked as she preened her two bulbous black eyes with her hairy black hooves. "Not very dangerous at all. I thought that you said that the child had been thrown off a cliff?" she added mischievously.

“He must have survived somehow your majesty” Raven replied nervously.

“Without any injuries at all, he must be tougher than he looks. Unless you’re lying to me of course.”

“I wouldn’t do that” Raven answered instantly.

“You had better not” she warned as acidic saliva dribbled down off her bony chin and melted a small hole in the honeycomb floor. “But they can wait for now, first tell me why you both failed to carry out the orders that you were given. After Flint informed me that Seaple was bringing in someone called Toby Smith from a planet called Earth I made it quite clear to you both that you either brought me the clock or made sure that he never left his own world, but you’ve done neither.”

“It was all her fault” Raven stated, as he pointed at his wife who was cowering fearfully at the back of the throne room.

Jumping up she ran forward crying “no it wasn’t you liar. You’re to blame for this mess.”

The stinger queen grinned saying sadistically. “Whoever is to blame will pay dearly, that’s for sure. But which one, that’s the question?” She slipped menacingly down from the door of her egg laying chamber and sat upon her black onyx throne. “But don’t let’s be hasty, that will all be decided in good time after you have both had an opportunity to speak. So come now, who will be first to put their case?”

Without hesitation, Raven’s wife threw herself onto the golden dais beneath the ornately carved throne. “I will speak first your Majesty, if you command me.”

“I do” the queen stated coldly, crossing her six hairy legs and waiting anxiously for the fun to begin.

“After I applied for the vacant head’s position at Smith’s school I brought my husband in as the new history teacher. I then gave the other Earth boy jungle juice and got him to attack the Smith brat so that Raven could save him and gain access to the clock, but he failed to get it and was thrown out. So I made him go back that night to steal it, but he mucked that up as well. As you can plainly see, I am not to blame for any of this mess. He is” she yelled, as she pointed an accusing finger at her ashen faced husband.

“Well” the queen demanded, switching her attention to Raven “what have you to say for yourself?”

“What can I say” Raven answered defiantly. “It’s all true what she says.”

His wife stared at him nervously, wondering what game he was playing.

He stared back at her confidently, like a cat stares at a mouse that it has trapped in a corner. “That’s why she is responsible my Queen” he cried. “Condemned by her own words. For she has freely admitted that it was her plan on both occasions. So I ask you who is really to blame, a mere soldier who only obeys an order or the general that gives him his orders?”

Enjoying the way that Raven had twisted his wife's words, and placed the blame firmly back onto his spouse. The Queen asked "well my dear. Your husband makes a powerful case, don't you think?"

Turning white, Raven's wife opened her mouth to speak but nothing came out of her quivering pale lips.

"I'm waiting" the stinger Queen said impatiently, taking great delight in watching the female before her tremble. "Come, come" she coaxed. "Surely there's something else that you want to say in your defence."

"I, I, I," came the stuttering reply. The frightened defendant searched for words to extricate herself out of her precarious position, "I, I,"

"Enough" screamed the Queen as she glided silently across the throne room and seized the petrified Mrs Raven by the shoulders. Thrusting her sharp stinger deep into her head she sucked out her lifeblood. Discarding the empty husk casually the bloodthirsty monarch approached Raven. "Don't be frightened" she laughed. "You know that it's quick, although very painful."

"Have mercy" he pleaded as he backed away.

"What's mercy?" she mocked as she kept coming forward with evil intent. Seeing Roland, who suddenly started crying in the corner. She stopped in her tracks asking "who's that blubbering wreck?"

Seizing the opportunity to escape his impending doom, Raven ran over and dragged the distraught schoolboy out from the shadows. "This is the other boy we spoke of. The one that we gave the jungle juice."

"Why did you bring him here, why didn't you just get rid of him?" she demanded. "Is he good sport?"

"Possibly" Raven lied. "Quite possibly, but in the mean time he has other uses.

"Which are?" the Queen asked suspiciously.

"The Smith boy will try and rescue him if he can. Even if it means putting himself in danger."

"Why would he do that?" she asked intrigued by the ridiculous prospect of one creature helping another.

Quickly reinforcing his point Raven responded "It's what humans do because they are irrational and weak."

"But I can catch that child out there and the old Sandman whenever I like" the Queen laughed, "we don't need this blubbering brat for bait." She moved nearer, raising her sharp stinger above her head as the desire for fresh blood surged through her again.

Intervening, Raven begged. "But we do need him your majesty. Just in case of any hitches. The sandman is more dangerous than he appears, and the child is the one that has been called to help the custodian. We still don't know why?"

Hesitating, she staved off her natural instincts as she pondered upon Roland's fate and Raven's council. Throwing her delicacy roughly aside she bellowed angrily. "Very well, let him live for now but guard this little sweetmeat well. Because I shall have some fun with them all later." She licked her lips in anticipation of the pleasure that awaited her. She mulled over the horrible ordeals that she would put them through before finally putting them out of their misery. Turning to the problem at hand she screamed. "But I won't wait for them to come here. Call out the entire hive and you bring them here to me alive. Take command Raven, but you'd better not let me down again because nothing will save you next time."

Running over to the doorway Raven picked up a large horn and blowing it he summoned the stinger squad leaders. "Get everyone into the air now" he screamed. "We go to capture our enemies."

"What's that humming noise?" Toby asked as he stood upon a rock studying tornados in the distance.

"I don't know" the Sandman yelled back cautiously as he cocked his ears and listened intently to the unusual sound. "But whatever it is, it's certainly getting closer."

"Well you'd better both hurry up and jump aboard because that's stingers that you can hear," a familiar sounding voice said from above.

Looking up, they saw Beearney hovering just above they're heads.

"Barn!" Toby screamed. "What are you doing here?"

The buzzer dropped down lower, until he was beside them. "When I awoke from my nap at the castle, a girl with green hair told me that you would be coming here, and that you may need my help. So here I am. But let's talk later because the stingers are getting close and that can only mean trouble. Get aboard and let's get out of here."

Without being told twice Toby and Grain clambered upon the hovering buzzer. But, as they climbed higher seeking a hiding place within the dark rain clouds, they spotted hundreds of angry stingers approaching fast. "It's a pretty big swarm" Beearney cried aloud as he accelerated towards cover.

"Have they seen us?" Toby shouted, trying to make himself heard over the rushing wind.

"You can bet on it" the buzzer answered as he decided against hiding and flew away from the oncoming insects.

Splitting into three groups, the main party of stingers kept chasing them while the two smaller parties broke off to flank them. Realising that they were being out manoeuvred, Beearney immediately pulled in his wings and dived into the valley below. Reaching the bottom in moments, he skirted along the rock strewn ravine precariously while his pursuers tried to cut them off in a pincer movement. Being considerably quicker and more agile, Beearney confidently out flew them by hugging the rough terrain at high speed. As the last stinger finally faded into the distance, the cocky little buzz-bomb slowed to a crawl. "How was that for low level flying?" he asked.

"Brilliant!" Toby shouted, feeling relieved that the immediate threat was over. "It's lucky for us that you came along when you did or it could have got very nasty."

"True" Grain quickly confirmed. "If it hadn't been for you I don't.. "

His words were cut short by Beearney suddenly swerving. As a large stinger shot past, just missing them with his poisonous sting.

"Sorry" Beearney shouted "it seems that we haven't lost them after all. It must be all the extra weight that I'm carrying because normally they can't keep up with me."

"What are we going to do?" Toby cried as the frightened buzzer lurched the other way violently avoiding a second deadly dose of stinger venom.

"We certainly can't out run them" Beearney responded despondently.

Toby felt the sandman instantly release his grip upon his waist. As he turned see what was happening behind him, Grain disintegrated and blew away in a cloud of golden dust.

"Nooo!" Toby screamed in desperation as the sandman float away on the breeze.

With the benefit of considerably less weight. Beearney nimbly side-stepped several more stingers using his new found speed. Putting several miles between them and their enemies, he stopped and hovered in cloud cover. "That was close" he whispered, scanning the sky for any sign of danger.

"It was, but what about Grain?" Toby asked.

"Don't worry about him; he can look after himself "Beearney answered. "Let's just keep quiet and hide in here until we are sure it's safe."

"Are you sure he will be okay?" Toby whispered.

"Of course I am" the buzzer lied.

Floating to the ground as a zillion minute particles of gently falling sand, Grain instantly shaped himself into a thin worm and worked his way beneath the sandy soil until he decided what was best to do. As he lay there, with one small telescopic eye protruding from the ground, he saw most of the stingers scatter in various directions as they continued their search. A few, breaking away from the main party flew back into the hive entrance which was situated within the side of the mountain. Determined to prove to himself that he wasn't a coward, he made his way slowly toward the home of his enemies. Reaching it quickly he slithered into the black opening. Seeing several guards just inside, he watched them as they marched up and down scanning the harsh desert landscape with their huge insect eyes. Grain watched the nearest Stinger, as his large mandibles continually flicked to and fro in a series of grossly exaggerated movements. "The queen is fuming" he said as he stared out into the barren wilderness. "That means that someone's going to pay."

"Who cares" another cackled, "as long as it's not me of course." Moving nearer the entrance of the great cave he added. “Don’t worry too much though, because she got that Earth kid to play with. He’ll keep her occupied for a while.”

“What do you mean?” the other guard asked “I thought that the kid got away on a buzzer?”

Patting his ignorant companion upon the back with his horny hoof, the first guard grinned showing two rows of needle sharp teeth. “That can’t be true can it, because old Starruptx here saw him inside didn’t you?”

“Yeah, I saw him,” Starruptx croaked, “and he was a strange looking thing.”

They got Toby, Grain thought. Leaving the guards still discussing the terrible fate of his little buddy he slithered off silently down the narrow corridor, deep into the hive below. Entering several of the hive’s many nurseries where thousands of eggs and pupae were developing, he searched for him in vain. He hid in shadowy corners as heavily armoured stingers ran here and there. As one stopped only feet away from him, he studied him carefully looking for any sign of weakness in his body armour. Nothing obvious, he stared up at his head which was wolf shaped with needle sharp fangs. He studied the wasp shaped body bearing the usual orange and black markings to warn his enemies that he was poisonous. Grain grimaced as he observed his six muscular legs and cloven hooves. Spotting its deadly stinger tucked neatly between its back legs, fear nearly took possession of him again. But, determined to not give into it, he slithered down even deeper into the hive until he reached the entrance of the throne room. He could hear the enraged queen as she bellowed angrily "So how did they escape?"

The Stinger that had led the second squadron visibly flinched as he answered timidly. "It was because of that buzzer turning up from nowhere and helping them my Queen. But it was Raven's squadron that let them slip by after we had flushed them out."

"Is this true?" she whispered, as she beckoned him nearer. "Did you let me down again?"

"Let me explain my queen" he pleaded desperately as he fell to his knees and threw himself upon her mercy. "I serve you as I served your Father I..." He stopped in mid-sentence as he felt a bony hoof press down hard upon his shoulders. "No!" He begged "Mercy, mercy."

"Mercy is for fools, death is for failure" she mocked as she drove her erect stinger deep into his back and sucked out his body fluids. Her hunger momentarily sated she floated back over onto her throne asking. "Why am I surrounded by such incompetence? Was it that which cost my Father Darvock victory? The constant failure of his pathetic followers? And you" she asked the trembling Stinger squadron leader. "Will you let me down as well? Because you have just witnessed what failure brings."

Dropping to one knee he bowed his head solemnly saying. "I can only guarantee, your majesty, that if I fail in any task that I undertake, you will not drain me dry as you did Raven. For I will have already fallen in battle."

"Good" she screamed "at last someone who understands the game. If you don't secure the victory, you do the decent thing and die trying. I want no more hard luck stories or whining. Get out there and find them or else! Take every drone in the hive with you. I want all three of them found and brought here now!"

Grain winced as the heartless stinger Queen sank her poisonous stinger into several unsuspecting guards for good measure. But he now knew that Toby and Beearney were still free. Although he realised that this was the perfect opportunity to regain his honour by helping the other child escape from under the evil Queen's nose. After waiting what seemed an age for the last of the stingers to leave, he began searching for the prisoner that he assumed was Roland. Just when he was nearing the point of giving up, he entered another nursery containing thousands of eggs and one sobbing prisoner who was sealed in an orange coloured egg chamber. Quickly forming himself into a crude saw, the sandman cut the terrified child free.

Tumbling from the egg sac Roland mumbled almost incoherently. "Thanks, but what's going on? Mr Raven has gone loopy and killed Toby. I tried to help him mister, I really did. But there was nothing that I could do to save him." His face turning white, he whispered "and there's an awful monster upstairs."

"I know about her, and you can tell Toby that you are sorry later" Grain replied.

"He's still alive?" Roland asked.

"Yes, he's still alive and kicking when I last saw him which is more than we shall be if we don't get out of here." Turning into a seven legged whiz cat, reputed to be the fastest land creature in the whole of zone, Grain purred "so hurry up and sit on because we've got to get going."

"I'm with you" Roland yelled leaping aboard the sandy coloured feline which quickly shot away into the myriad of honey coloured tunnels. They ran at a fast pace at first, until nearing the Queen's chamber room. Slowing to almost a walk, the muscular cat padded along silently. Reaching the wide doorway Grain peeked around the corner to make sure that it was clear. After giving it the once over, they sneaked quietly past the opening. As they turned the corner Grain stopped dead in his tracks, as he saw the stinger Queen waiting for them.

"Well, well what have we got here" she chuckled. "An old sandcastle carrying an overweight sweetmeat." Moving quickly to the centre of the corridor she blocked their path as she crouched menacingly, ready to fight.

Their only way of escape cut off, Grain set Roland down quickly, telling him "if you get a chance to run, take it." Facing the malevolent striped fury before him, he tried to gain an edge, "do you know who I am? I'm the one that killed you're Father, and I'll kill you to if you don't get out of our way."

Enraged by the threat from her Father's Murderer, the Queen lunged forward with her lethal sting, but missed. The agile sandman neatly slipped to the side. Again she thrust her lethal abdomen forward, like a fencing master looking for an opening. But, once more Grain ducked and dived as he danced with her needle of death. The raging Queen, becoming even more desperate she sprayed him with acid, hoping to disable him. Doing his best to ignore the burning liquid, Grain formed himself into a thick battering ram with legs and ran at his foe hitting her in her left eye.

"Bzzzzzzzzzz!" She screamed aloud as the unknown feeling of pain shot through her head. "Bzzzzzzzzz!" She shrieked again as the encouraged sandman struck her again in the other eye. Stabbing blindly, she tried to skewer her foe again but only struck air as he nimbly moved around on tiptoes. Seeing the opportunity to finish her off once and for all, he quickly changed into a large fist. His hand stayed by pity, he became a whiz cat again. Picking up a Roland, he jumped over her and sprinted for the exit while she continued screaming in pain and stabbing the air blindly. Reaching the hive entrance quickly the whiz cat and his bewildered rider shot between the startled guards and ran for their lives. Several high flying stingers circling overhead, saw them and gave chase. "Hold on" Grain shouted to his frightened passenger as s he reached top speed over the rugged terrain...

“Where are we going?” Roland asked as he held onto the bounding animal’s flowing mane.

Grain responding breathlessly. “We’ll make for the secret door, it’s our only chance.” Lengthening his stride, he tried to gain ground on their pursuers. But, hearing the shrill buzzing sound of angry stingers, he knew that they were gaining on them. Reaching the bottom of the mountain leading to the portal he bounded upwards, to find the door ajar.

“Come on slow coach, we’ve got the air from the tornado and we’re only waiting for you” Toby shouted.

Diving in without hesitation and sliding to a halt, Grain shook Roland off his back and snapped the door shut! Changing into a chimpanzee form he took Toby in the arms saying “thank goodness the door was open because half the stinger army are after us.”

“While the other half have been chasing us!” Toby exclaimed.

“Can they follow us through here?” Roland asked nervously.

“Not until they discover how to open the doorway” Grain replied. “But who knows how long that will take them?” Grain noticed that Toby was looking over his shoulder at Roland. He stood aside, so that they could talk together for a few minutes.

“I think I owe you an explanation” Roland whispered quietly as the new door into the distinctive planet of Quasi opened.

Without waiting for the others Beearney glided out into the welcoming warm air of the arid desert.

He left Toby and Roland sat together with attentive sandman listening with great interest.

Roland grinned stupidly "now look here Red." Correcting himself, he said "sorry, I mean Toby. Now you and I have never really got to know each other have we? Well I understand that I may have made it a bit awkward for you when I kept on about your ginger hair. But let me tell you straight, I never really meant you any harm."

"So why did you try to strangle me?" Toby asked as the grim memory came flooding back.

"I don't really know" Roland responded, as he fidgeted uncomfortably. "When Mr Raven first suggested it, I said no way. But he just kept on about it all the time. After a while it seemed like the right thing to do. Especially after he told me that you were calling me a fat pig behind my back."

"I didn't" Toby complained bitterly. "I never called you anything. Even when some of the other kids at school called you Tubs behind your back."

"Well I didn't know that did I. Anyway I wouldn't blame you if you did, after the way I treated you" Roland admitted.

"Did anybody give you anything to drink?" Grain asked curiously.

"Miss Blakelock and Mr Raven gave me green lemonade" Roland replied, "why?"

"Probably had jungle juice in it" Grain whispered. "It's what unsavoury types normally use when they want to control someone's mind."

"I remember seeing a red light in Roland's eyes as he tried to throttle me" Toby cried, "and in

Raven's as well. Hey! Come to think of it the head offered me green lemonade in her office."

"That confirms it a red glint is one of the commonest side effects there are."

Roland looked out into the desert wilderness. "You must really hate me" he said miserably. Feeling a small hand gently touch his shoulder, he knew that he had chance to make amends.

Grain watched the two of them as they talked together about their families. Deciding that it was better if they did not dwell there too long he interrupted their heart to heart saying, "that's enough of that mushy stuff. You'll be seeing them all soon enough anyway if everything goes to plan. Not only do we have to be going, I'm just dying to know how you managed to get some pure air, when I've still got this." Taking his hand out of his small pouch he held out the second collection phial in his long wrinkled fingers.

"Come here please Barn," Toby shouted. The buzzer landed beside them. "Right Grain," Toby said. "Take out the stopper of that little bottle and put it up to Beearney's lips so that he can blow into it."

"Why?" Grain asked, puzzled by the request.

"Just be patient and you'll see" Toby answered.

Holding the phial steady Grain watched the grinning buzzer blow into it with a short, sharp breath.

"Quick cap it!" Toby screamed, clapping his hands together in delight.

"Once more doing as he was asked, Grain pushed the leather cork firmly into the collection phial. Noticing a tiny bright light inside it he said "what's this?" thinking that it was about time that he was let in on whatever it was that was going on.

"That my friend is pure air from the centre of a twister" Toby replied. "Me and Barn collected it after you abandoned ship."

"Are you sure?" Grain asked as he scrutinised the contents closely.

"Of course we're sure" Toby assured him. "After you left, Beearney and I stayed in the thick cloud for a long time until we thought that the Stingers had gone. But, as we came back out to look for you, they attacked us again from above. Now, because we were much lighter without you, Barn was able to out manoeuvre them fairly easy at first but as he started to tire, they kept coming at us in waves. It was only a matter of time until one of them got lucky and stabbed us with his stinger but this plucky little buzzer took them for a ride through twister territory. He scared me half to death as well I can tell you as he flew close to those spinning tunnels of death and destruction." Beearney grinned smugly as Toby continued to tell the others about their daring exploit.

"When we approached the first twister there must have been about fifty stingers on our tail."

"Only fifty?" Beearney quizzed the story teller.

"Well a hundred then" Toby responded apologetically as he quickly returned to telling his story.

"More like five hundred I thought" the buzzer interrupted.

"All right Barn, five hundred, a thousand. Now if you're happy, I'll finish telling Roland and Grain what happened." Winking cheekily he added "if that's all right with you of course?"

"It is" the buzzer replied quietly.

"Anyway as I was saying, there we were with all these blimming stingers chasing us so Beearney decided to give them a roller coaster ride to remember. Getting as close to the tornados as possible, he drew them in close. Then as the twister changed direction, Barn would shoot away leaving the stingers caught in the edge of the back draft. Being larger and a lot slower than he is they got sucked right into the vortex. Again and again he repeated this death defying stunt while I held on grimly and prayed for it to end. When the last stinger was either destroyed or disabled, I breathed a sigh of relief thinking that the danger was over but old Barn here had other ideas. As he shot straight up into the heavens like an arrow, I thought that he was going to take me right up into space, but suddenly stopping he shouted. "Hold on tight because now we are going to get some air."

"I looked down, seeing the Mother of all twisters beneath us." His face growing pale, Toby took a deep breath. "It was humungous and spinning like a demented top as it cut a huge swathe of destruction across the landscape."You gotta be joking" I said "why does it have to be this one, let's pick another."

But I couldn't get him to change his mind. "If you want the purest essence of wind" he argued. "Then we have to get it from the biggest and fastest twister."

"Are you sure?" I implored him, hoping that he'd reconsider. Ignoring me though he dived down towards the top of it at speed. I shut my eyes at first and just held on. But as we got nearer and accelerated, I opened them just enough to take a quick peek as we entered the eye of the storm.

Down and down we went into the raging beast of nature as she reaped havoc upon anything unfortunate enough to be in her path. As we descended lower though into the swirling vortex, a light appeared which was intensely bright, although minute in size. As I was gazing at it in wonder, Beearney just scooped it up into his mouth. What was so amazing though was what happened next."

"What was that?" Grain asked impatiently.

"The twister just dissipated, while shooting us out like a bullet from a gun."

"Remarkable" Grain remarked smugly. "Nearly as remarkable as how I rescued this chap from the stinger Queen."

"No way!" Toby cried, as all the attention suddenly switched to the grinning chimpanzee.

"That's a story for another day" the beaming sandman whispered, tapping his slightly upturned nose knowingly. "Because first we have got to decide what happens next, and about what to do about Roland."

"I assumed that he'd be going with us" Toby responded. "Especially as we're friends now."

"Does he want to go?" Grain asked "and is he a liability?"

Toby looked over at Roland, who was looking lost. He thought that it was probably better for everybody concerned if he could go home but he didn't know if that was even possible, what with the gravity machine being damaged. Plus Beearney was just too valuable to spare as a taxi back to Seaple's castle. No, his class mate would have to come along with them whether he wanted to or not. With that in mind he said, "what do you think Ro?"

Looking apprehensive, Roland held out his hand in friendship. "Well my life hasn't really been that good up to now has it. What the heck, count me in because it can't get any worse can it?"

Chapter Six
The Fountain of Zurs

They followed the natural path through the ever shifting sand dunes although they had absolutely no idea where it led and after several hours of walking and seeing nothing but giant prickly cactus and the odd lizard, Grain called a halt so that they could decide what to do next. "Are we going to just keep walking without knowing where we are heading?" he asked.

"What else can we do?" Toby replied as the burning hot sun continued to beat down upon them unmercifully.

"Can I make a suggestion?" Roland enquired sheepishly...

"I don't see why not" Grain answered, sitting down beside him.

" Well as we probably won't last more than a few days without food and water, why can't Toby and the buzzer fly, while you and I run along behind."

"I can't carry you around for long spells" the sandman answered quickly. "Besides I haven't got very much beach world water left, and I don't know how any other salt water will affect me. I need to conserve my energy, although this sun is helping."

"We're all not fed by the sun and sea like you Grain" Toby said. "But you've gone and made me feel thirsty now, with all this talk about food. So, I'm going to have a nice cold drink of cola."

"Where from?" Roland asked as he licked his dry cracked lips.

Jumping up immediately Toby ran over. "Crikey I forgot all about you. How long is it since you had anything to eat or drink?"

"I've had nothing since yesterday" Roland replied. "So where's this cola that you got stashed away?"

Taking the remaining sea cherry from his pocket. Toby held it in the palm of his hand saying "you swallow this and I'll show you." As Roland reached out to take the unexpected offering, a sandy coloured hand shot out and snatched it.

"What are you doing?" Toby demanded. "Give that back, Roland needs it."

"That may be true" Grain readily agreed. "But should we let him have it, that's the question?"

"Don't be daft" Toby responded instantly "he's desperate."

"I know that, and I realise that his life probably depends on his having it." He hesitated, "but is that what's best for our mission? If the cherry you have taken suddenly stops working, what happens then? Do you starve to death before you have the chance to fulfil our quest?"

Standing up to his full height Toby eyeballed the sandman as he exploded in an out of character torrent of anger. "You may be prepared to let Roland die, but I'm not. You can forget all about keeping the last cherry as back up, because I don't need it, Roland does. So give it back now so that he can have a drink."

"What if" Grain started to answer

But he was cut short, as Toby bellowed "now!"

Grain reluctantly passed the precious cherry to Roland, who looked at it suspiciously. "This isn't cola" he cried despondently. "This is only a stinking little tomato." Standing up he tossed it as far as he could throw it.

"Noooo!" Toby screamed as it disappeared somewhere in the distance.

Unsure why his classmate was making such a fuss about nothing. Roland only flopped back down upon the sand.

"You stupid fool!" Grain shouted angrily as he scurried off to look for it.

When the sandman returned sometime later with the cherry, he found an informed and excited Roland, eagerly awaiting his arrival.

Once more he reluctantly handed the cherry to the thirsty schoolboy who devoured it immediately. As Toby and Grain sat down together to talk privately they could hear his loud groans of pleasure.

“Was that wise?” the sandman asked.

“Probably not, but it was the right thing to do” Toby replied.

“I suppose it was” Grain agreed. “But let’s hope that the cherry that you took keeps working. Because there’s no food out here in the desert.”

Toby stood up and stretched, feeling tired. Deciding that it would be better if they kept moving, he called Beearney over and slid gently upon his back.

“Oh well, I suppose that I will have to do it” Grain moaned unhappily as he reshaped his form into a carbon copy of the buzzer. “Come on” he yelled to Roland. “Let’s get on with it, if we must.” As a very contented and even more portly looking Roland waddled over. Grain wondered just what he’d let himself in for.

When Beearney took to the air, he couldn’t help but snigger at Grain who was carrying far too much baggage. As they gained height they could see the lie of the land and realised that if they’d just followed the desert track, they would have just gone around in endless circles. Content in the knowledge that their chance of success had vastly improved, they headed toward the setting sunset with renewed hope.

As the first weak rays of daylight illuminated the land far below, they couldn’t believe their eyes. Under the cover of night, the arid and sandy terrain had changed into one of many rocky granite out crops which developed into a harsh grey land of broken stone. But, spurred on by their desire to find the third element, they headed toward the red sun until they spied a sinister looking shape in the distance. Reaching the hideous looking fortress that resembled a long buried maggoty skull, they landed upon the uneven patch of ground in front of it. Asking Beearney to look around, they nervously waited, until he returned looking unhappy.

"What's up?" Grain asked immediately.

"We're here, it's Zurs" the buzzer mumbled."

"Zurs, what's that?" Toby asked innocently.

"You're sure it's the fountain of dreams?" Grain demanded.

"Yes" Beearney replied.

"Is there any sign of fresh water springs nearby?" Grain asked hopefully...

"No" the buzzer responded.

"But what is it?" Toby cried, "this fountain, what is it?"

"It's a place where nobody returns from" Beearney whispered, "and the one place that no one would choose to go."

"That's why I was banking on there being a pool, or spring outside" Grain added.

"So what do we now?" Beearney asked.

"Let's go and look for some water somewhere else" Toby suggested.

"We can't do that" Grain mumbled. "Because it's not very likely that there's any water in a place as dry as this. We haven't even seen an oasis have we? While legend say that this is the place where lost souls makes the water sweet, so it's more than likely that we shall find what we need inside."

"Well that settles it, if we can't go back; we might as well go forward. Toby argued, so if you are all ready we should press on."

Grain stared at his young companion and nearly bursting with admiration he declared proudly. "Toby, whether you were selected for this quest rightly or wrongly. I must say that it's been an honour for me to accompany you. You have been a true hero on this trip. Brave, resourceful and the perfect travelling companion. So, whatever fate awaits us inside this horrible place. I want you to know how I feel."

"Wow Grain, that's really nice of you to say that. I'm the one that should feel privileged being here with you three. Oh, and don't let's talk like it's the end because it's not, it's just the beginning. But before we enter this place you had better tell Ro and me all that you two have heard about it because it may help."

"Very well" the Grainster whispered nervously, "but you're not going to like it." He took a deep breath and spoke quietly. "It's said that this place was built by the Gods at the beginning of time, to protect their treasure. As the tales of great wealth became exaggerated over the centuries, thieves from all over the zone have come here to try and steal it. Its common knowledge anyone who that nobody has tried, has never returned. An old Sage from the planet Chavillex claims to have seen inside this place in her dreams. If she's right it really is a terrible place for she said that she saw tunnels with devious defence mechanisms and rooms full of deadly traps. There was much more of course, but that's all that I can remember."

"What about the flaming arrows and hot tar" Beearney said.

"They've got the general idea" Grain said sternly, kicking the buzzer on the leg.

"Killer bats and tattooed warriors" Beearney added.

"That's enough" the sandman whispered between his teeth, as he kicked him harder.

"Oh, I see, yeah, sorry." Beearney said, finally catching on. "Don't take any notice of me because I don't know what I'm talking about. I mean who would ever believe that there are warrior maidens carrying poisonous blow pipes..."

"Will you just shut up?" Grain shouted angrily. "Because no one really knows what's in there do they. It's just idle speculation and an old woman's rambling."

"I suppose so" Beearney agreed quickly as he tried to repair some of the damage that he'd caused.

Taking the Sandman by the shoulder Toby said. "If we're going, let's go now, before we change our mind."

Grain only grinned in answer, as he followed the brave little hero from the planet Earth.

As they neared the foreboding fortress, the skull's mocking grin seemed to broaden as it welcomed them, with the promise of death.

"Here the door" Beearney whispered quietly, "through this missing tooth."

"Looks nasty" Roland remarked.

"It sure does" Grain agreed.

Facing the new challenge that awaited them, Toby tried rallying his companions as they fought with the fear of uncertainty. "Yes it does" he said bravely, "but it may not be as bad inside. Just remember how all the wood folk feared Bradollbecknat until they actually met him. It may not as grim in here as we actually think it is, so instead of standing here worrying about it, let's just go and see what it's like."

"Okay little warrior" Grain said nervously. "Let's go and see what fate has in store for us this time."

Taking the initiative, Toby walked toward the doorway while his three nervous companions followed behind. Reaching the entrance he found that he was unable to see inside. "It's too dark" he whispered, "we shall need some kind of light so that we can see where we're going." He jumped back in shock as several bright lights suddenly flared up inside illuminating the enormous cave with their flickering golden flames.

Grain looked uneasy, "that's to let us know that we are being watched" he whispered. "So let's proceed cautiously."

"Sounds good to me" Beearney responded, taking a quick glance over his shoulder.

"We're all gonna die!" Roland yelled as he suddenly panicked and tried to run.

Grabbing him by the collar Grain said firmly. "Stop and think about it before you go. For there's nowhere for you to go, is there unless you want to go and get lost in the burning desert by yourself? So be a good lad and get a grip of yourself because you're coming in here with us whether you like it or not."

Letting go of Roland, Grain expected him to try and run again. But he was pleasantly surprised when the shivering schoolboy only answered hoarsely "yeah, you're right."

"Good for you" Toby said taking a small step through the rotten tooth. Moving forward carefully, he made his way further into the great big space while the other three watched and waited by the doorway. "Come on in, there's nothing to be frightened of " he yelled.

Chewing on his large rubbery lip, Beearney flew in first and hovered suspiciously. While Grain who had slipped in behind him, hugged the wall for cover.

Realising that the Sandman was correct about the futility of running away. Roland entered as well, albeit reluctantly. Hearing an ear shattering rumble behind them they turned to see a solid slab of stone slide over the doorway with a loud thud! "We're trapped!" Grain cried.

"We're doomed" Roland answered.

Now with nowhere to go but forward, the four friends made their way over to the large stone staircase and started climbing while keeping a look out for the unexpected. Nearing the top of the staircase without incident, Toby stopped abruptly.

"What is it?" Grain asked "why have you stopped?"

"I've got a bad feeling" Toby answered as the hairs on his neck stood on end.

"I can't see anything to be scared of" Grain responded.

"I know that" Toby whispered "but I, I ..." The stairs suddenly levelled out and they all hit the flat surface hard and started sliding back down. Reacting instinctively, Beeaney scooped up Roland who was closest to him and hovered while Toby and Grain plummeted back down at speed.

Grasping a thick stone spindle with one hand the quick thinking Sandman grabbed a hold of Toby with the other. Holding onto him firmly he shouted out "take a look down there."

Toby stared down at what moments ago had been a solid stone floor, and couldn't believe his eyes. He looked down into a deep dark pit full of sharp spikes. In shock, he turned to look up at his saviour who was still gripping him tightly.

"It's all right" Grain yelled, "I won't let you go."

Dropping Roland off at the top of the stairs. Beearney flew back down and picked up the still trembling Toby who stood in silence. Meanwhile the versatile Grain made his way back up in the form of a large stick insect. Changing back into a chimpanzee he noticed that Toby was staring into space. Determined not to let him dwell to long upon their near disaster, he loped over to him saying firmly “okay, time to go.”

“Give me a minute” Toby pleaded.

Knowing that they weren’t safe while they remained in the fortress, the sandman answered gruffly “all right. But the sooner we get the water, the sooner we can get out of here.”

“If we ever get out” Roland moaned miserably. But seeing Grain glaring at him he decided not to say any more.

Leaving the other three together to collect their thoughts, the Sandman walked a little way ahead to see if there were any other traps near. As he turned a corner into an adjoining corridor he stopped abruptly as an angelic voice asked him cordially. “Why do you try to steal that which belongs to the Gods?”

Seeing a silver robed creature with a cherubic face, Grain replied automatically “we don’t. We only want some water.”

“Why?” the creature asked.

“To save the universe” Grain responded.

“It’s still stealing, whatever the reason” the pale creature stated.

“I suppose so” Grain agreed reluctantly. “But sometimes you have to do things that are wrong, for the greater good.”

“The end justifying the means?” the saintly looking figure suggested. “But as the keeper of this sacred place. I must warn you that I am entrusted with the solemn duty of punishing all thieves. I have been doing so for several thousand years, but if you go back the way you came, I will spare your lives."

"We can't, we need the water" Grain said. "So can't you just give us a thimble full and we will be on our way."

"I cannot do that" the creature said, "go back or you die."

"But we don't want the water for ourselves Grain shouted angrily. "It's to save the universe damn it!"

The creature smiled once more saying softly, "Gods own the universe and will do with it what they will." His pleasant smile becoming a sickly red mask of death he faded into thin air, leaving the Sandman shaken. Determined to not frighten the others even more than they already were, Grain decided to keep the strange visitation a secret. "Ready to go on now?" he asked as he rejoined the others.

"As ready as we shall ever be" Toby responded.

"Good, then let's be off" Grain advised. "But keep you're eyes peeled."

Taking the sandy coloured chimp by the hand. Toby held it as they started walking. As they turned out of the tunnel Toby felt Grain suddenly tighten his grip.

"Are you okay"? he whispered.

"I'm fine," Grain lied as he felt a cold chill run through his entire body.

Moving on for several hours without resting, the four companions seemed to make good progress until Beearney stopped dead in his tracks. “We've been here before” he said. “I remember this torch on the wall, it's slightly crooked.”

“Are you sure?” Grain asked.

“I am” Beearney responded.

Grain walked over and examined it closely. “Well I certainly can't remember it; they all look the same to me. What do you think?” he asked the two boys. Receiving no reply from them, he turned around to find them both staring at something in the corridor. What's the matter?” He asked in alarm.

“Insects” Roland mumbled, almost incoherently.

“Where?” Grain asked.

“Up ahead” Beeaney whispered.” Can't you see them all huddled together?”

Staring down into the long corridor the sandman looked again, but saw nothing. “No” he answered glumly “I can't see a thing. We sandmen have poor vision.”

“What shall we do?” Roland asked, “go back?”

“That's not an option” Toby chipped in.

“What is?” Roland asked, getting irritated.

“That's still to be decided” Toby said firmly, taking command of the difficult situation.

“But as we know that we can't go back. It's just a question of how we are going to go forward. Any ideas?” he asked hopefully.

“Maybe we can fly over them” Beearney suggested, “it's a pretty high tunnel.”

“Possibly” Toby said “but they may be able to fly or jump. We need to find out if they are dangerous?”

“How do we do that?” Roland asked.

Grain walked off purposefully toward the crouching insects stating determinedly. “If someone has to go and take a closer look at them, it might as well be me. You stay here until I return, whatever happens.” Changing shape into a seven legged whizz cat he ran down the corridor at speed until the blurred image of three large brown scorpions became clear. Slowing his pace just a little, he decided to try and take them by surprise. Changing into a giant pair of scissors upon two thick legs, he ran at them snipping for all he was worth.

Separating quickly the three heavily armoured scorpions prepared to do battle. “Shrhh” they hissed defiantly as they raised their sharp pincers to protect themselves. Dodging the middle insect’s thrust agilely the sandman cut off one of its pincers and slid beneath its soft underbelly where he drove his two sharp blades deep into its flesh. “Shrhh” it wailed in agony as it reared up in pain. Without hesitating the elusive Grain rolled out from under it and stabbed it again. Floundering helplessly in its death throes it reared up once again before crashing to the flag stone floor. Using several small eyes Grain watched the other two deadly insects carefully but was caught off guard as a giant stinger struck him hard in the chest with a lightning thrust. He gazed in horror as an orange liquid bubbled out of the gaping hole and started burning him. "Acid" he yelled as he blocked a second vicious strike from the other circling beast.

Deciding that the best form of defence was to attack, he rolled again and cut three legs off a scorpion in a single motion, as it teetered precariously beside him he dived beneath it and repeated the same process as on the first. Bending his knees, he forced his two long blades upward, into his shrieking adversary. Rolling from beneath it athletically, he faced the last one as it snapped at him ferociously with its giant pincers. Again and again he avoided its deadly stinger, looking for an opening but no matter how he tried, he couldn't get in close enough to reach its weak spot. Realising that he was tiring badly, he turned himself into a javelin and propelled himself at his gladiatorial foe. However he bounced harmlessly off of his impenetrable armour. He knew that he had to get underneath the scorpion to kill it. But how, that was the question, now that he never had the element of surprise. So, forming into a hard ball, he threw himself at the creature, trying to knock it off its feet. But he was flicked away easily by its formidable pinchers.

"Shrhh!" The angry beast screamed in pain as Beearney butted him hard from the side. "Shrhh!" It shrieked again as the buzzer quickly repeated the treatment. Seizing the opportunity created by the surprise attack, Grain reformed into scissors, and sprinting hard he drove his two long blades into the distracted scorpions exposed belly.

"Shrhh" it squealed as it was impaled from below. No matter how it tried it couldn't reach its attacker who was being protected by its own great bulk. "Shrhh" it gurgled softly as it staggered and fell with a loud thud upon the valiant Sandman. Toby and Roland ran forward as the floundering giant finally became still, and tried lifting the dead scorpion off their friend.

"Quick Barn" Toby pleaded "let's get this ugly thing off him." They all shoved and pushed for all they were worth but realised that there was no way that they could move something so heavy. "How can we move it?" Toby yelled. There was no easy answer as there was nothing around to work with. "Come on think" Toby urged them "there must be something that we can do to get him out from there?"

"What though?" Beearney asked. "Because we can't dig him out, not through solid stone?"

"No we can't, but there has to be something that we can do to help him" Toby protested.

Moving closer Roland suddenly cried "maybe there is a way." Walking between the other two dead creatures he carefully picked up a severed stinger. With a smile upon his face he came back to where the giant lay. "I don't know if this will work or not but as we are desperate we can try it."

"Try what?" Toby demanded immediately.

Holding out the still twitching sting before him Roland whispered. "On a wildlife programme I watched about scorpions, they said that even in death its poison is so potent that it can still cause death or violent convulsions. So if we stab this sting into the scorpion that's on top of Grain maybe it will move enough for us to pull him out?"

"Will it work?" Beearney asked.

"Possibly" Roland answered, "or we could flatten him some more."

"But the scorpions dead" Toby mumbled miserably.

"Yes its dead all right" Roland responded. "But its nervous system may still be functioning."

"Is that possible?" Toby asked.

"I think so" his classmate replied.

"Do it" Toby said "and let's get ready to pull him out if it works."

Without hesitation Roland thrust the sting into the soft tissue of the scorpion. "It's twitching" he shouted.

Toby watched in disbelief as the gigantic carcass momentarily trembled, then stopped. "Do it again!" He yelled, "do it again!"

Roland drove the sting in, and again the creature trembled, this time more so. As a small space appeared beneath it, not thinking about his own safety, Toby dived headfirst into the tiny opening.

"Quick!" Roland cried to Beearney "let's shore up this side for as long as we can."

Joining Roland the buzzer wedged his chunky body beneath the still shaking monster.

"Hurry up!" Roland shouted "it's heavy."

Toby crawled back out from beneath the monster, carrying a flattened Grain draped over his hands. Placing him gently upon the ground he asked him “are you okay?”

“Not really” came the mumbled reply as Roland and Beearney leapt clear from the creature as it crashed to the floor.

“What can we do?” Toby asked.

“Nothing” Grain answered feebly, “unless you have some sea water from beach world on you.”

Toby searched for a way that they could help the sandster but with the last of the sea cherries gone, he just couldn’t think of anything to try. Turning to the others he hoped that they had an idea. But as he stared into their expressionless faces, he realised that they had no suggestions either. “No!” He screamed in terror as he saw Grain disintegrate into a pile of sand before his eyes.

“It’s too late” the buzzer said sadly, “he’s gone.”

“He can’t be” Toby screamed, “he can’t be.”

“But he is” Roland said sadly “and we can’t change it. So we had better get moving before any more scorpions appear.”

Turning upon Roland, Toby yelled angrily. “I don’t care about scorpions, I just want Grain back.”

“I know you do” Ronald whispered. “We all do, but it’s not going to happen is it.”

“How do you know?” Toby demanded.

“My Mother never came back” Roland countered quickly.

Toby looked up into his class mate’s face to see that he was also crying and he realised that he wasn’t the only one that was hurting. He picked up the small bag containing the elements that they had already collected. Opening it carefully he checked that the two phials were undamaged. “Yeah” you’re right” he agreed as he wiped away his tears. “But I’m not leaving him here on his own. So let’s work out how we can carry him, because I want him to be buried back on beach world.”

Beeaney revealed a small furry pocket in his side. “I’d be honoured to bear him” he said sombrely.

Scooping up the pile of lifeless sand gently. Toby let it slide between his small fingers into the secret place, and walked over and kicked the scorpion that had robbed him of his friend. As he walked away sulking, his two companions followed in silence.

They trudged wearily along the never ending corridor as it wound deeper into the heart of the mountain. Each footstep becoming harder as guilt and sorrow weighed heavily upon them.

“We should have helped him quicker” Toby moaned.

“We didn’t know that he was going to rush in like that” the buzzer argued “and even if we had, could we have reacted any sooner?”

Toby stopped and turned to look at Beearney. “I think that he wanted to prove to himself that he wasn’t a coward” he said.

“Why?” the puzzled buzzer enquired.

“Because he froze momentarily when we went to see the ogre.”

"We all freeze at times" Beearney responded, "that doesn't make us cowards. Anyway he was the bravest little creature that I ever met, even if he never knew it himself."

Taking Toby by the elbow and Beearney by the wing Roland whispered softly. "If you want to really know how brave he was, let me tell you about how he saved me from the stinger Queen."

"He never did tell us that story" Toby said sadly.

"He didn't want to ruin Beearney's big moment with the twister" Roland answered.

"I'm not surprised at that" Beearney said proudly. "Although he was small in stature, his heart was as big as a lion's."

As the trio of broken hearted travellers moved off, Roland told them about the defeat that the crushing sandman had inflicted upon the Stinger Queen.

"Why didn't he finish her off?" Toby asked.

"Who knows" Roland replied philosophically. "Perhaps it was his humanity that stayed his hand."

"But he wasn't human" Beearney interrupted.

"You know what I mean" Roland replied awkwardly.

"We do" Toby answered proudly. The corridor suddenly turned sharply and they were confronted by a deep chasm which had an old rope bridge spanning it. Moving to the edge, Toby looked down, seeing nothing but darkness. "Wow! This is deep" he said as he moved back quickly.

"It sure is" agreed Roland, who suddenly felt dizzy.

Gripping the nearest handrail of the bridge Toby shook it and was pleasantly surprised to see that it felt sturdy. "It seems okay" he suggested.

Taking to the air Beearney hovered above the bridge as he inspected it thoroughly. Suddenly buffeted by fierce winds he returned to them saying "where did that come from? it nearly blew me into the rock face."

"But is the bridge safe?" Toby demanded...

"It looks it" the buzzer confirmed, "are we going to cross?"

Toby smiled, trying to look confident but he was fooling no one with his little charade. It just didn't make any sense to provide a safe way over a deep chasm, for someone that you were trying to kill. Having no choice in the matter, they began walking out onto the gently swaying bridge. With each step they took, the feeling grew that they were making a big mistake. Reaching the middle, a flaming arrow shot past Roland's face and fell into the abyss below. "Crikey!" He screamed as he ducked down, seeking cover. Seeing several more arrows heading their way, he was quickly followed by the others. Peering over the flimsy handrail Toby saw several grey creatures who reminded him of rooftop gargoyles. Firing another volley of burning missiles at them, they hovered upon their grey pointed wings.

"Duck!" Toby yelled, avoiding another arrow that shot between the narrow gap in the ropes and stuck in the bridge. Knowing that they had to get over to the other side as soon as possible. He cried "let's make a break for it." He jumped up and ran for his life while numerous burning arrows whined through the air. Feeling his feet upon firm ground, he spun around to see the large frame of Roland lumbering towards him as fiery arrows peppered the burning bridge around him. Gritting his teeth he finally made it to the end of the bridge where Toby dragged him to relative safety. Seeing that Beearney was burning in a ball of fire. He yelled "I'm coming" as he leapt back upon the bridge and started running back. Met by a searing wall of flame though, he was driven back. "Barn!" He cried out as the flaming bridge suddenly collapsed and fell into the depths of the dark chasm below. Staring down into the emptiness, he realised that Beearney was gone.

"What do we do now?" Roland asked, "because there's no way that we can go on by ourselves."

"Of course we can" Toby snapped! "We have to or it's all been for nothing."

Roland grimaced, "you're right" he said. "But it would have been better if it had been me that had copped it."

"Don't say that" Toby whispered softly. "For our time will probably come soon enough." Something shiny appearing in the thick cloud of swirling smoke, he hoped that it was Beearney arising like a phoenix from the ashes. His fleeting hope cruelly dashed, he saw that it was only a small glass bird flying toward them. Almost hypnotised by its beauty, he watched it as it came nearer. Suddenly gathering speed, he realised that it was coming straight at them. Standing up he yelled “quick, take cover.” As his classmate awkwardly pulled himself onto his feet. The crystal bird shot over his shoulder and hit the wall, smashing into a thousand pieces. They ducked down, as the deadly shards of razor sharp glass fell all around them. Still cowering with fear, Roland stared down at the shattered remnants of the bird. “Blinking heck!” He shouted “that stupid thing nearly hit us.” Noticing that Toby was staring at something behind him, he turned to see a large flock of the birds hovering in formation. “What are we going to do now?” he asked, as his legs started shaking.

“The only thing we can do” Toby responded “run!” Turning as one, they sprinted down the corridor as fast as they could knowing that there probably wasn’t anywhere to hide. But spurred on by their will to survive, they ran as fast as their legs would carry them. Running around the corner Toby glanced back to see several of the birds accelerating towards them. Pulling Roland into the wall, they overshot their intended targets and shattered harmlessly against the stone wall. Leaping over the remains of their broken bodies they ran again until being halted by a large hole in the floor which covered the entire width of the corridor.” There’s no way around!” Roland screamed as two more birds, just missing them shot past at speed.

"Then we have to go down" Toby yelled as he grabbed Roland's arm and tightly and pulled him into the large black hole.

"Aghrr!" They screamed as they plummeted down into the enveloping darkness. Picking up speed rapidly they continued to fall, until suddenly slowing down. They softly touched down upon a hard stone floor. Momentarily unable to speak because of shock, they both stood there in the darkness numbed by their frightening experience and by the fact that they were still alive. Seeing a dim light in the distance Roland shook himself free of his stupor and put out his hands in front of him as he tried to locate his companion. "Are you okay?" he panted breathlessly.

"Yeah" Toby answered automatically as he too, groped around in the gloom, "you?"

"I'm okay, I think" Roland responded. "But why aren't we dead after falling all that way?"

"Beats me" Toby sighed.

"Talking of beating, I ought to beat you good and proper" Roland growled. "For dragging me into that blooming great hole. You nearly frightened me to death you little plonker." Knowing really that the action had saved his life, he laughed nervously, adding "but thanks anyway."

"Anytime" Toby murmured, as he too spotted the faint orange light that was shimmering like a beacon of hope through the darkness. "We'd better go this way" he said as he slowly fumbled his way towards the amber glow that beckoned them.

"Suits me" Roland whispered, as he followed closely behind. Steering a course toward what they hoped was somewhere to rest they realised that it was farther off than they had thought and they knew that if there were any unseen traps or sudden surprises in their path that there was just no way they could avoid them. So trusting to luck, they shuffled one foot in front of the other. Making good progress, Toby tried taking their minds off their tragic loss. "How's the sea cherry, does it taste as good as I said?"

"It's good" Roland responded. "But I don't really feel like eating right now. It's unusual for me really, because normally I eat all the time. That's why all the other kids call me Tubs behind my back."

"That may be true" Toby answered honestly. "But if you weren't so mean all the time they probably wouldn't call you anything."

"Maybe not" Roland agreed, "but it's too late to worry about that now because we aren't going to get out of this mess anyway?"

"Let's just wait and see" Toby responded. "They haven't been able to kill us yet have they."

"Just give them time" Roland laughed sarcastically

As the light got closer it cut into the darkness like a powerful torch beam giving the two fast growing friends a bit of a lift. "Not far now" Toby whispered as he wondered what lay ahead.

"No not far" Roland replied nervously. "It looks like a doorway" he added apprehensively.

With the last clinging remnants of darkness finally banished, the two frightened schoolchildren entered into an illuminated chamber. "Good grief!" Toby exclaimed as he studied a mountain of gold and jewels that were heaped into several large piles. Turning around to ask what Roland's thoughts were, he found that he had vanished. "Roland!" He shouted "where are you?" Receiving no response from him, he called out again. "Roland, are you there?"

"No" the soft voice behind him answered, "he is not."

Spinning around Toby stared directly into the face of the angelic looking creature that had challenged Grain earlier. "Where's my friend?" Toby asked.

"He's over there with the other thieves" the keeper answered as he pointed to Roland and Beearney, who were frozen within two large blocks of ice. Alongside them was a small pile of sand.

"Let them go!" Toby shouted.

"Why should I?" the being asked nonchalantly.

"Because they deserve to be free" Toby replied.

"But they're dead" the creature reminded him cruelly.

"Roland's not" Toby argued.

"Of course he is" the grinning creature insisted.

"How can he be?" Toby demanded. "He never died, he survived like me."

"He never" the creature gloated. "He never survived the choice of the Gods."

"What does that mean?" Toby blubbered.

"The choice of the Gods, it's quite simple really." He smiled as he toyed with his unwelcome guest. "They ordained long ago that if anyone ever reached the treasure held within this place, no matter how many of them there were, only one would be left unharmed. All others would be taken as payment for the sacrilege committed against this house of Deities.

"That's not fair!" Toby cried. "Why take Roland instead of me?"

"Does it matter?" the keeper asked. "For you really only want the treasure don't you. So take whatever you want and leave."

"I don't want your stinking treasure" Toby yelled defiantly. "I want my three friends back."

Looking confused by the concept of someone not wanting to help himself to as much booty as they could carry the custodian eyed Toby with great interest. "Is it your decision not to take anything from this holy place? What about the valerian necklace, it's priceless? Or the blood red ice crystals from the planet Squidish, they are one of a kind?

Becoming angry Toby marched forward. "Don't you understand, I don't want any of your treasure? We never did, any of us. We never even wanted to come here. But we had to because we needed some water, water of the finest quality so that we could repair the gravity machine and save the solar system."

"Everyone comes here to try and get the treasure" the keeper responded, looking somewhat confused.

"We never!" Toby shouted adamantly.

"Well that leaves me in a very difficult position" the creature said. "Because this is most unusual, for not only are you the first group of beings to ever reach the inner sanctum, now you claim that you do not want to take any treasure. These are circumstances that were never allowed for in my instructions. I need to decide what to do about this unusual situation." Without waiting for a reply he faded into thin air, leaving Toby alone with his thoughts. Walking over to his friends he stared at them in turn. First Roland who looked like he was sleeping peacefully. Beearney was burnt and shrivelled almost to the point of being unrecognisable. Finally he stared down at the small pile of golden sand that had been his beloved sandster. Feeling lost, he wept for his three companions who had been taken from him in such tragic circumstances. He was still crying when his angelic looking host reappeared. "Child I have been most impressed by you and your friends willingness to face danger to help others. I also feel that such bravery should be repaid in some way so I have decided to give you the opportunity to restore life to your three companions. There is always the danger of course that you may forfeit your own life instead."

"I'll take that chance!" Toby stated defiantly.

"You don't know what you have to do yet" the creature said.

"It doesn't matter" Toby declared, "I'm doing it anyway because I can't leave here knowing that I could have helped my friends."

"Brave words indeed" the keeper responded. "But let me tell you first what you will have to do to save them. Then if you still wish to still try, I will let you. Although I believe the chances of you surviving the ordeal are virtually nil."

"I'll take that chance" Toby replied.

"Very well" his host proclaimed as he bowed low. "Come and be the first outsider ever to see the magical fountain of Zurs."

Leaving the others behind Toby followed the strange and somewhat frightening custodian as he floated out of the room and back into the corridor. Stopping almost straight away, he beckoned him nearer.

Moving closer, the floor beneath them started sinking. "What's going on?" he shouted as they slowly descended through the thick stone floor.

"Patience" his host whispered softly. "For if you fail the test of Zurs your soul will be remain here forever."

Whatever was going to happen would do so whether he liked it or not. Toby thought as they descended into enchanting world below. Which was illuminated by a multitude of shimmering torches that swayed this way and that in a rhythmical dance. Becoming dizzy, Toby nearly toppled from the small platform but a strong hand gripped his shoulder and steadied him. He managed to regain his balance as their tiny elevator silently reached the lower level. Floating away from the lift the creature approached a tall cylindrical glass sphere that was full of thousands of small lights that were darting here and there as if they were alive. Moving closer, the custodian fell onto his knees and started chanting.

Toby waited until he finished his prayers and approached him. "What's this glass thing called?" he asked.

"Behold the magical fountain of Zurs. Made by the Gods long ago, it has the power over life and death. If you are brave enough, skilful and extremely lucky, you may just succeed in bringing your friends back to life if you are sure that you want to risk losing your own. It is also the sacred place where the first water sprang forth to breathe life into a dry and lifeless universe."

"What have I got to do?" Toby asked as he stared wide eyed at the myriad of flashing lights shooting around inside the container.

"Simple" the custodian replied "you see all the lights that are kept within the fountain of Zurs. Each one is the soul of a being who has desecrated this sacred place. Your three companion's souls are now in there as well. To free them from their eternal punishment you need to do is dive in and find them. If you are successful in your task, they will be restored to life. If you fail, their souls will remain here forever. With one other, yours."

"How do I work out which ones they are?" Toby asked.

"With bravery, skill and luck" the custodian smugly replied. "But because you are so young I will give you one piece of advice. Choose carefully because at first glance they all may look the same, but they are not."

Toby took a deep breath; he knew that he didn't want to accept the challenge that awaited him but knew that he had no choice, as it was his friend's only chance of life. "Okay I'll do it" he stammered nervously, "how do I get inside?"

"I'll show you" the keeper declared. Snapping his fingers, a glass staircase slid silently out of the wall.

Toby climbed quickly, while his nerve held out. Reaching the top of the stairs he hesitated as he stared down into the swirling mass of rising bubbles and light. Shutting his eyes he sucked in as much air as he could and plunged down into the crystal water. He concentrated upon the moving spheres of light. Which ones are they? he thought as he quickly sank down to the bottom. Knowing that he'd only be able to hold his breath for a couple of minutes, he was shocked to see a glass lid sliding over the top of the tank, trapping him. I'm done for now he thought as a sandy coloured ball suddenly caught his eye. Although there were many balls that looked similar, this one seemed bitty, almost sand textured. So, swimming after it, he grabbed it and studied it as it rested in the palm of his hand. Although his choice wasn't really based upon logic, he somehow knew that this was the soul of the sandman. Keeping a tight grip upon it, he looked around for any other lights that had any characteristics similar to either Beearney or Roland.

Spotting another sphere nearby he swam towards it as fast as he could. Only to see it carried away upon a stream of bubbles. Darn it, he thought as he pursued it once more. But again, as he closed in, it was gone, lost within the myriad of speeding balls of light. Seeing it shoot to his left he chased it again, but this time as he neared it he guessed that it would be swept away on the ever changing currents. Anticipating its change of direction, he stuck out his hand and grabbed it before it could disappear again. Once more the overwhelming feeling came over him that this was Beearney. Although it was predominantly orange in colour, like many others, it had a very faint pattern of black rings. That's two of them he thought as he let out a long string of air bubbles. Watching the pearl necklace rise to the surface he realised that he couldn't hold his breath much longer so he swam back up to try and get a mouthful of air. But there wasn't a pocket of air between the close fitting transparent cover and the water surface so with his lungs nearly bursting, he tried not to breathe as the invasive liquid forced its way into his mouth and throat. Panicking and thrashing about he struck the glass lid in desperation but was unable to break free of his watery prison. The last few bubbles leaving his lips, he thought that he was going to drown, but didn't. His mind raced back to when he had tried to escape Drucilla and her big needle. A big grin spread across his face as he thanked his lucky stars that Grain had caught him before he could get away. Still laughing to himself about that awful, but wonderful experience, he dived back down, seeking the third coloured ball that could be Roland's soul. However, he couldn't see anything that reminded him of his classmate's personality. He grasped the nearest one to him and held it in his hands to study it until the sandy coloured sphere bumped it hard sending it back into the fast flowing maelstrom of water. "Wow Toby thought, they're trying to help me. Taking another sphere he replaced the one that had been rejected. That dispatched too, he took another at random. Again it was rejected with a sharp bump! Standing upon the base of the tank he started catching more but they were also spurned by the sandy coloured globe. Although he was becoming tired and feeling somewhat dizzy, he grabbed another and placed in with the others, expecting it to be also rejected. But to his surprise the three spheres of light just nestled together in his palms. Hoping that he had selected the right balls he headed wearily back to the surface. The glass barrier slid open as he approached it and he climbed out and sat upon the edge, holding the three precious orbs in his hands.

"Good, at least you managed to collect three" the custodian said. "But are they the right three that's the question?"

"I don't know" Toby mumbled nearly inaudibly as a jet of liquid shot out of his mouth. Breathing with some difficulty, he sent another shower of fluid into the air, then another, as his body readjusted and his breathing became more stable.

"I didn't realise that you could breathe in liquids." His host stated as he took the three balls of light and examined them carefully.

"I didn't know that I could either" Toby answered.

The keeper looked at him sceptically. "Now let's present these to the alter of Zurs and see if you have passed the test." Whirling around on his heels, he slid effortlessly over the cold stone floor into another corridor while a wet and exhausted Toby shuffled along behind him. Entering another door the guardian ceremoniously bowed before a large shrine which was draped with exotic flowers and bowls of fresh fruit. Bowing a second time, he knelt before the altar and placed the three glowing spheres upon it. Toby trembled, as much from the fear of failing, as from the cold, as the guardian held out his hands and start praying. One of the balls rose into the air and the smiling face of Grain momentarily appeared upon it before it faded into thin air. Another ball floated up and hovered as the first had done. The fleeting image of his friend Beearney materialised, but it too was gone as quickly as the first. As Toby tried to take in what was happening, a third sphere quickly followed suit. He stared at it as the chubby face of Roland appeared and winked at him before fading as the others had done before him.

Rising from his knees his host cried out “praise be to merciful Zurs.” He swept by Toby who was still shivering in his wet clothes. Once again Toby found himself trying to keep up as his stony faced host sped back down the corridor to where they had left his friends. Entering the room quickly the custodian hurried over and touched the small pile of sand gently. A white light radiated from his fingers and swirled in the air momentarily before entering the remains of the sandman. Toby watched in silence as his smiling friend came back to life. Moving to Beearney the creature repeated the action to restore the once badly burned buzzer. Touching Roland in the same way, his classmate yawned as he awoke from his imprisonment. The keeper waved his hand, freezing them again.

“What are you doing?” Toby shouted angrily. “I thought I passed the test?”

“You did” the creature replied. “But do you really want me to restore these three miserable creatures back to life when I can offer you so much more?”

“Of course I do” Toby protested.

“If that’s what you want, fine, I’ll do it.” The grinning custodian whispered. “But before I do, let me tell you what I can give you instead.” Clicking his fingers, Toby felt the clothes he was wearing turn dry.

“A mere parlour trick” the keeper cried, “what do you really want? let me see now.”

“I want my friends back as you promised!” Toby shouted.

“You shall,” the custodian answered. “Unless I can tempt you with something else of course.”

“Why can’t you just do as you said you would?” Toby asked.

“Because I do not want to lose these three souls unless I have to.”

“Why don’t you want to set them free?” Toby asked nervously.

Moving closer the creature whispered quietly. “Because no one has ever been allowed to leave this place before.”

“That doesn’t matter” Toby argued, “because a promise is a promise. Or at least that’s what my parents say.”

“Are they the ones that raised you?” the keeper asked.

“Yes” Toby responded, as his voice dropped an octave.

“Where are they now?” the guardian asked.

“Back on Earth” Toby replied sadly.

“Are you sure?” the keeper responded quickly. “If that’s the case, then who are those two behind you?”

Looking over his shoulder Toby stared into his Mother’s face. “Mom!” He shouted as he ran into her warm welcoming arms.

“Are you okay?” she asked him as she gathered him into her ample breasts.

"I am now" he whispered, "how did you get here?"

"Well it's hard to say really dear, because there I was one minute doing the ironing while your Dad was watching the news to see if there was anything about." Hesitating momentarily, she added "you."

"Are you okay Son?" his Father asked.

"I'm fine Dad," Toby replied "although I missed you both terribly."

"I bet you did, but its okay now that you can come home" Mr Smith responded cheerfully.

"How?" Toby asked "how can I come back home while the whole universe is in danger of being enslaved?"

"It's not your problem any more as this nice man here will tell you. For he has told us if you leave with us he will fix everything."

"Including freeing my friends?" Toby asked suspiciously.

Toby's Mother looked at his Dad. "Well everything but that, because he wants them to stay here."

"What so that their souls can float around in a blinking goldfish bowl for eternity?"

"It's a crying shame, I'll give you that" his Mother admitted. "But you would be able to come back home, isn't that what you want?"

Becoming angry Toby turned his back upon the two beings claiming to be his parents. "Go away!" he yelled defiantly as tears ran down his face. "You're not my parents. They'd never ask me to betray my friends. Nor would I, at any price." Standing as tall as he could he eyeballed his host angrily. "If you've finished playing your silly game now. I'd appreciate it if you would free my companions."

"Very well," the custodian declared finally accepting defeat. "Let it be so," and snapping his fingers once more. Grain, Beearney and Roland all awoke again.

"Wow what a scary dream I had" Roland said as he yawned and stretched.

"Me too" Beearney answered, "I think I was some kind of fish."

Ignoring their comments Grain quietly told toby. "I think we had better go now while we still can. I get the feeling that this strange creature hasn't finished with us yet."

"Strange?" the custodian cried. "Strange, after I warned you about entering this holy place and offered you the chance to go back. Resurrected three of you from oblivion and gave him the opportunity to go home." Pointing at Toby, his eyes bulged as veins started appearing on his forehead.

"It's only right that you brought them back" Toby shouted. "you that killed them in the first place. As far as going home's concerned, yes hopefully I will. After I have repaired the gravity machine."

His cherubic face becoming a mask of contorted demonic rage. The angry custodian yelled "although I have to reluctantly let you and your pathetic friends leave, you will leave here empty handed. For I will not let you take any sacred water with you."

"But we need it!" Toby cried as his frustration got the better of him.

Ignoring his request the sneering custodian vanished through the door which quickly shut behind him.

"What do we do now?" Toby cried as he clenched his tiny fists in anger.

"We get out of here now" Grain responded. "Before that angel of death returns." Taking the other door he ran out into the corridor and started running, with the others close behind.

"Why do we need to run?" Toby asked breathlessly. "He's agreed to let us go."

"Just keep going" Grain responded as he encouraged them to go faster. Before they had gone very far though, Roland started to tire badly. Scooping him up in his arms, the sandman ran on. Following his example, Beearney gently nudged Toby with his snout as the grateful schoolboy clambered aboard his hairy back. He accelerated to keep up with the sandman, who was going faster than ever. Entering yet another corridor they kept up the relentless pace.

Leaning forward upon the buzzer's neck. Toby asked "but why are we running?"

Twisting his muscular neck the bee-horse replied "I don't know why Grain's is in such a hurry. Perhaps he's afraid that the custodian will go back upon his word?"

Hearing a scream of outrage from the depths of the mountain temple, the sandman urged the buzzer to go faster as they headed up a long steep incline.

"Does he know where he's going?" Toby cried as the buzzer glided around the latest corner.

"Who knows, but he seems to know where he's heading" Beearney answered.

Seeing a doorway just ahead the four companions kept on making for it as the terrifying cries got closer.

"We've done it!" The sandster yelled as they rushed outside and were greeted by warm sunlight. Stopping a short way from the doorway, he turned to look back at the foreboding hole. Squinting hard in the bright light of day, he saw the custodian who was watching them from inside.

"Come back" he cried, "you have what belongs to the Gods."

"What does he mean by that?" Toby asked curiously. "We never took anything did we?"

"Oh yes we did" Grain corrected him "we took this." Reaching over and taking his small pouch from around Toby's neck, he took out the third glass phial from its small leather pocket and pulling out the stopper. He held his other hand over the opening and squeezed hard. Tiny drops of water formed at the tips of his fingers. They slowly dripped into the container until it was nearly full. "There" he declared triumphantly "sacred water from the fountain of Zurs."

"How?" they all asked in unison.

The Grainster changed into his favourite shape, that of a chimpanzee. "Well let me try to explain to you as best as I can. Although I have been around for a very long time. I still do not know why some things happen to us Sandmen. But, one of the strangest things that happens to us, is when we become something else. We sometimes inherit the characteristics of that entity, and when we return to our original form small traces of what we were, can remain in our bodies. That's the way that we can grow, not in size, you know but physically. In spirit, or in character if you prefer. But this time a new phenomenon has occurred. For since being trapped within the magical waters. I feel different, stronger, and even perhaps younger which I can only put down to water retention. After all this wasn't just any water that we were immersed in was it? It was the holy water of Zurs for goodness sake." Putting the tiny glass phial carefully into his pouch he said solemnly. "Although I find its properties invigorating. I have happily given up most of it for our quest."

"Most of it?" Toby asked cheekily.

"Yes, most of it" the sandman replied as he blew a kiss toward the red faced custodian who was still standing in the shadows watching them. Swaggering off into the desert, Grain swivelled his head around to warn the others. "Oh and let's keep a look out for stingers because they're sure to be on our trail."

"Blimey" Toby mumbled "I'd forgotten all about them." Their spirits were soaring after collecting the third element and refreshed by constant cold drinks and fast food. The two schoolboys talked and got to know each other a little better and were pleasantly surprised to find that they had quite a lot in common. Promising each other that they would remain friends if they ever got back home, they sang songs as they followed the rejuvenated sandman and sap happy buzzer. Reaching the spot where they had entered the desert world, Toby pressed the button upon his armlet and within seconds the door slid silently open that would lead them to their next destination. As they scampered through the yawning gateway, they wondered how hard the last trial would be...

Chapter Seven
Dragon Fire

Taking Grain aside Toby talked to him quietly while Beearney and Roland scouted the surrounding area. “How do you feel? you seem different” he asked.

Putting an arm around him the sandster replied. “I’m not surprised, because I feel like I did when I was young.”

Toby nestled into the sandman’s comforting shoulder. “That’s good” he answered, “but don’t change too much because I kind of like you the way that you are.”

Grain ruffled Toby’s unkempt red hair. “Don’t you worry old Grain won’t change. What’s wrong, you seem worried?”

“I am” Toby replied as he dug his heel into the lush green grass.

“What’s troubling you?” Grain asked sympathetically.

"Everything's going crazy."

"How do you mean?" Grain asked.

"Old Seaple's ill for a start and we don't know if he will survive do we?"

"True" the sandman agreed. "But we can't worry about him for now. We must concentrate upon our mission. Because, if we can't repair the gravity machine, it won't matter if he recovers or not. The zone will come to an end as all stars and planets collide. Although I don't think that he's been the same since he defeated Darvock. Winning that battle took its toll upon him. In fact, his magic has almost diminished now altogether. Between me and you, he told me only the other day that when he pulled you through that old clock, it took him two days to recover. Likewise when he created that old man that gave your Father the clock."

"That old man wasn't real?" Toby asked.

"Only in your Father's eyes."

"Wow!" Toby exclaimed. But do you think that Seaple will really get better?"

Grain looked pensive, "I don't know. But I'm hoping that because he and the gravity machine are connected, if we can cure one, we will also cure the other."

"I hope that you're right" Toby said.

"Anything else worrying you?" Grain asked.

"There is actually, my Mum and Dad. They must be worried sick."

"I expect they are" the sandman responded. "But remember if we save all the creatures in the solar system, that includes them."

Toby coughed and cleared his throat as his emotions came to the fore. “Yeah I know, but I miss them.”

“I know” Grain replied.

Toby coughed again, and this time it sounded throatier. Grain felt his body shake violently as he coughed and spluttered. He was worried about the child that had become like another split to him. For Drucilla had told him that one of the first signs of the vaccines wearing off was persistent coughing. Deciding to keep his suspicions to himself, he said nothing.

“Roland told us about your fight with the stinger Queen” Toby said.

“He had no right to” Grain responded angrily as his stony face broke into a hint of a smile. “I was good though, as I dodged her poisonous sting.”

“Why?” Toby asked.

“Why what?” Grain replied.

“Why did you take such a risk?”

Grain laughed automatically, sending his booming laugh for several miles. “I thought that it was you that she had ready to skewer.” His grin changing to a frown, he added. “But I would have gone in anyway, even if I had known that it was Roland being held prisoner.”

“I know that Grain, but why do it at all because you’ve got nothing to prove to me or the others.”

“Maybe not” Grain replied, “but maybe I have something to prove to myself. For when I went to war I was fearless in battle, but when we approached the ogre's house I became frightened for the first time."

"So you fought the stinger queen and three giant scorpions to prove that you are still brave?" Toby asked immediately.

"I suppose so" Grain admitted.

"Well don't do it again and that's an order" Toby said firmly.

"Affirmative Boss" Grain responded with a grin.

A short time later Beearney flew in with Roland. "Everything okay?" he enquired as he noticed that Toby was coughing.

"Everything's fine" Grain lied. "Although Toby's caught a little cold."

"Nothing serious I hope?" Beearney asked.

"I don't think so" Grain responded. "What did you discover upon your little surveillance mission?"

"I don't really know where to start" Beearney cried "there's so much to tell."

Grain held Toby a little tighter, as another bout of coughing made him go red in the face. "We don't need all the details" he snapped. "Give us the short version."

Sensing that something wasn't quite right. Beearney answered the irritable Sandman quickly. "Just around this canyon there's a small village that has a run down inn. Roland and I popped into see what we could find out about the area."

"I get the picture" Grain interrupted angrily, "now get on with it."

"Okay, okay, no need for that grumpy" the buzzer complained. I'm telling you what we found out as fast as I can."

Realising that he'd been wrong to criticise the little buzz bomb, Grain apologised. "Sorry, sorry I didn't mean that. But we really do need to get on."

"Apology accepted" Beearney said. "Now as I was saying before I was so rudely interrupted."

"Don't push it" the sandman warned.

"Right" Beearney said as a big beaming smile spread across his face."Where was I, oh yeah. The inn, well anyway the Freshnite that runs it told us that the dragon's lair is a little way north of here."

"How far?" the sandman demanded.

"About twenty miles," the buzzer responded as he continued to wonder just why Grain was so jumpy.

"Let's get going straight away" Grain ordered.

"Can't we rest a while?" Roland pleaded, as he slipped off his trainers. "Because my feet are killing me."

"I'll be killing you in a minute if you don't get up and get moving" Grain yelled angrily, as his pent up emotions finally exploded.

Moving between the irate sandman and the stunned schoolboy. Beearney stated clearly "you two stay here while Grain and I have a little chin wag. But keep your eyes peeled for stingers, because there are signs that they are about."

As they walked away, Toby started coughing again.

Seeing Grain look back anxiously. Beearney guessed that whatever was the matter, it concerned Toby. “Right” he demanded, as they stopped about twenty metres away. “Why is he coughing so much?”

Grain looked back, making certain that they weren’t being overheard. “Look Beearney” he said apologetically. “I’m sorry that I bit your head off just now, but I’m worried.”

“I know that” the buzzer responded, “why?”

Grain checked again to see if the two schoolboys were listening to them but seeing them chatting together, he continued in hushed tones. “The vaccines enabling him to breathe are running out, and when they fail altogether...” He paused as the words stuck momentarily in his throat. “He’ll suffocate.”

“Sqeeeeeesh!” Beearney exclaimed, as he swore in his native tongue of buzzeree. “What can we do about it?”

Putting out a warm sandy hand the sandster strongly gripped Beearney’s horny hoof, stating defiantly. “We can get the dragon fire and get out of here quick.”

“Right” Beearney agreed, “Let’s get the others ready and fly.” As they turned to rejoin the others, Grain stopped in his tracks. “Did you feel something pass by?” he asked.

“Yeah” the buzzer answered as he sniffed the air suspiciously. “What do you think it was, there’s no wind?”

"I have an idea what it is" Grain replied. "Because I remember something similar happening once before but we have enough to worry about for now. So don't mention it to the others and I'll deal with it when it becomes a problem. Now let's get moving as time is of the essence."

Reaching the others Beearney shouted "come on lazy bones, get your shoes back on, we have got to be going."

"You changed your tune" Roland moaned as he put on his trainers.

"That may be so" Beearney answered. "But times a wasting, so move it or else!"

Toby stood up as another coughing fit started, after clearing his throat he wearily made his way over to the buzzer. "I hope we're flying" he said weakly as he clambered aboard the buzzer and held on tight.

"It looks that way" Beearney chuckled.

"Here we go again" Grain moaned as he became a second buzz bomb. Not waiting to be asked, Roland leapt aboard causing Grain to stumble slightly. "Hoy!" He shouted angrily. "Just take it steady I'm not a moon mule you know."

"Sorry" Roland apologised, as he tried to get comfortable.

"And don't fidget" Grain added miserably.

"I won't" Roland cried as he continued squirming around.

"Quiet!" Beearney suddenly yelled.

"Why?" Roland asked.

"Shut up!" Beearney and Grain shouted in unison.

"What's that rumbling sound?" Roland whispered. "It's like a delicate sound of thunder."

"No it's not!" Beearney shouted "its stingers!"

Without further discussion, Beearney took to the air and headed north while Grain and his passenger flew close behind. "They're getting closer" Grain yelled as he came alongside the speedy buzzer.

"Too close for comfort" Beearney replied. "Let's dive and do some low level flying before they spot us."

"Okay" Grain cried "but remember that I'm only a learner."

"That's a deal" Beearney said as he dipped a wing and shot down to ground level. He effortlessly skirted over trees and hills as they tried to reach the dragon's lair before being detected while the honorary buzz bomb followed clumsily in his wake. "Look up" Beearney cried as he turned sideways to fly between two large pine trees.

Copying the buzzer's manoeuvre, but with much more difficulty. Grain stole a skyward glance to see an army of stingers high up in the clouds. There must be thousands of them up there he thought as he followed the accelerating buzzer through a series of tight twists and turns.

"Just a little further" Beearney shouted as he slowed and hugged the green terrain even closer.

"Good!" Grain yelled, as he narrowly avoided a sharp tree branch.

"There it is, there's the cave" Beearney shouted.

Reaching it quickly, they slipped inside and waited anxiously to see if they had been spotted. Toby, feeling unwell, leaned against the wall and retched violently.

Grain rushed to his side and patted him gently upon the back. "That's a nasty cough" he said sympathetically. "But don't worry we will be back in Seaple's world before you know it."

Hardly able to catch his breath Toby mumbled. "I hope so because I feel rotten."

Realising that he was living on borrowed time Grain ordered "let's go and find this dragon." Moving as fast as they could they made their way into the heart of the mountain. This time though it seemed considerably hotter than the last time. With sweat pouring off the two children and the buzzer overheating, they pushed farther into the stifling darkness that the dragon Scarfle called home. Before they had gone very far Beearney stopped and wiped the sweat from his fuzzy face. "It's getting hotter" he suggested, as he pointed at the two flagging boys.

Grain saw them both slumped against the cave wall with exhaustion and cursed. "Drat it, you're right, it's much too hot for them in here. One of us had better take them back to the mouth of the cave, where it's cooler while the other one tries to get a free sample from the dragon."

"But who does what?" the rapidly dehydrating buzzer asked.

Seeing that Beearney wasn't fairing much better than the others, Grain decided that it was best that he continued on, while they returned. "You take them back" he ordered. "I'll join you as soon as I can."

"How are you gonna get fire alone?" Beearney asked.

Scratching his chin the sandman replied with a grin "I don't know, I haven't thought that far ahead. But don't worry, I'll think of something."

"Don't go in alone" Toby shouted as he staggered over.

"Sorry" Grain replied softly. "I know that I promised you that I wouldn't do anything stupid again but this time we don't really have a choice. This intense heat is too much for all three of you whereas I don't really feel it as much."

"I don't want to leave you" Toby pleaded.

"I know that" he whispered, "and I don't want to be separated from you either. But it's the only option that we have."

"I suppose so" Toby reluctantly agreed. "But you take care of yourself and hurry back as soon as you can."

"I will" Grain promised as he kissed Toby's cheek, and left to seek out Scarfle. Running along the corridor he fingered the small specimen glass and said to himself "this is for Toby."

Some time later, spotting the remains of a badly charred carcass, he slowed his pace and proceeded more cautiously. While the stifling temperature in the cave continued to rise.

"Boring" a deep voice mumbled miserably from around the corner. "Trying to sneak up on an unsuspecting dragon like that."

Freezing in his tracks Grain took a quick peek around the rugged rock face to see a large green dragon sitting upon an enormous pile of burnt armour and charred weapons. What now? Grain thought, knowing that he'd lost the element of surprise.

"Are you going to come out and introduce yourself or not?" Scarfle the dragon asked. "Because I like to know who I'm barbecuing."

Taking another quick look, Grain saw that the dragon had two blood red eyes, which were both firmly focused in his direction. While his slightly open mouth clearly showed two rows of razor sharp white teeth. He ducked back behind the cover of the thick rock.

"Well come on in and introduce yourself. If you are brave enough to come in" Snarfle suggested.

"I haven't made my mind up whether to or not yet" Grain shouted back as he tried to work out what was best to do.

"I won't hurt you" Snarfle cried.

"How do you work that out?" Grain asked.

Snarfle laughed cruelly, sending a shiver throughout the sandman's entire body. "When you can generate as much heat as I can, it's pretty quick to roast somebody. So I wouldn't think that it would hurt too much."

"That's very comforting to know" Grain responded as he tried to figure how he was going to get close enough to get some of the dragon's fire without being turned into piece of Kentucky fried chicken.

"Come out, come out where ever you are?" the giant lizard mocked. But Grain had made his mind up that he was going nowhere until he had formulated some sort of plan. Sending an eye on a stalk around the corner he took stock of the situation but couldn't see any way to gain an advantage now that the creature knew he was there. Thinking of all the different forms he could take, he tried to find one that would help him get close enough to get a sample of fire, without being burnt to a crisp. Although he wasn't sure whether speed, brute strength or the ability to fly would be best.

"I'm getting bored" Snarfle called, trying to encourage his latest visitor out into the open. "Well at least answer me, if you intend to remain in hiding" he added mischievously.

Grain took a deep breath and replied "My name is Grain Sandy Sea bottom and I am very pleased to meet you."

"That's better" Scarfle mused "I love chatting before supper."

"Supper?" Grain asked stupidly, as he was momentarily caught off guard.

Old Snarfle laughed again, making the Sandman tremble with fear again. But now that he had regained his confidence of old, he knew that he wouldn't run, no matter what. It was just a matter of how best to proceed. But he knew that while he wasted time talking to the dragon, Toby would be getting worse. Deciding to find out how fast Snarfle's reactions were, he started waving his telescopic eye about to attract his attention.

Not wanting to disappoint his visitor, Scarfle sent a short blast of blue flame and sizzled the eyeball.

"Ouch!" Grain yelled as he sampled the full extent of his adversary's power.

"Pretty hot eh?" Snarfle cried, "but it gets hotter, the angrier I get. Now are you going to come out and talk or are you going to hide back there like a coward?"

Grain grimaced as the cheap jibe made him angry. But he knew that the dragon was just trying to tempt him out from his position of safety. He stared down at his charcoal grilled eye that was black and still smouldering. "What can I do?" he thought as he ransacked his brain for an answer. Feeling his small satchel move, his hand shot to where the collecting phials were but he found that one of them was missing, the empty one. Looking down by his feet he expected to see it on the floor, but it wasn't there. He checked his leather pouch again, but the pocket was still empty. "Where, how?" he thought as a sudden movement close by caught his attention. His mouth dropped open with shock as he watched as the glass collection container floating behind the dragon. "What the" Grain whispered to himself as he followed its progress through the air. "What do I do now?" he asked himself. "For I need that bottle to save Toby." Without hesitating, he prepared to make the ultimate sacrifice for a friend. The cunning Sandman changed into a Transmoultian screech bird and glided around the corner into full view of Snarfle.

"About time" he said as he licked his lips in anticipation. "I was starting to think that you were going to remain in hiding forever."

"No" Grain answered in the scrawny bird's high pitched voice. "I was just preparing myself.

"What with stuffing?" the sniggering dragon replied." There's no need for that because I'm not really that fussy about what I eat."

Hoping that an opportunity would present itself Grain responded. "But if that's the case why didn't you eat the poor creature that was toasted just outside the doorway?"

"He's too far away for me to reach" Snarfle said sadly as he reflected upon the missed meal. "He wasn't fast enough to out run my flame though." Forgetting his former victim, he concentrated upon the strange looking creature stood before him. "What are you?" he enquired "some kind of bird?"

"Does it really matter?" Grain responded, "If you intend to eat me anyway."

"Yes it does actually" Scarfle replied. "Because although I eat virtually anything, I like to keep a record of each species that I devour."

"Why?" Grain asked morbidly.

Crossing his two scaly front legs the dragon grinned, "nosey little thing aren't you."

"Well?" Grain asked impatiently as he watched the small glass bottle floating in the air just behind

Scarfle's head. "Before you eat me, the least you can do is answer a simple question or two."

"True I suppose" the beast answered, as he studied the odd looking species before him. "If you were as big as I am" he said, "and had been trapped within this mountain for a thousand years, you would also try to relieve the boredom a little if you could. For what is there for me to do in a place like this? Nothing, so I keep a record of all the different species that wanders in here accidentally or come to try and kill the last great dragon. Before I fry them into a piece toast, of course." He snorted, sending a thin yellow burst of flame into the air. "The only other thing that I can do to relieve my boredom is warm up the rock with my fire which I do quite often, as it gets rather chilly in here."

Grain laughed, sending his ear piercing screech echoing throughout the mountain.

"What's so funny?" Scarfle demanded, "answer me or I will fry you alive."

The sandman stopped laughing and walked closer to the dragon. "It's funny don't you think? Here you are one of the most feared and powerful creatures in the whole zone, and you're stuck in this mountain because you're too fat to get out."

Scarfle glared at the impertinent creature before him and was about to blast him into eternity when Grain added, "and here you are about to eat the only creature that can free you?"

"What do you mean?" the dragon asked, sucking back in the flame that he'd just been about torch his impudent visitor with.

“Do you know who sandmen are?” Grain enquired.

“No, who are they?” Scarfle demanded irritably.

Changing into a four tailed Dipper the Sandman said calmly. “They are a race that can change their shape at will, and I happen to be one of them.”

Snarfle was astounded by the creature’s ability to change his appearance but was impatient to see how it affected him, or why it was so funny.

“I” Grain continued “can become anything that I want.”

“So?” the dragon cried, nearing the end of his patience.

“It’s simple” Grain said “if you give me some of your dragon fire, I will release you from this prison.”

“How?” Scarfle asked, suddenly becoming interested again.

“Like this” the sandster replied as he reformed his body into a stone cutting machine. “Now watch this” he said as he moved to the wall of the cave and cut a large chunk of rock.

“Pretty impressive” Scarfle admitted, as he saw the possibility of his finally escaping. “Then I can resume eating every remaining creature upon this horrible little planet and after I have gorged myself upon their flesh, I can move on to somewhere else.”

Grain retook his favourite form, that of a chimpanzee. “Why would you want to do that?” he asked.

"Because that's what I do, eat things."

"Without a thought for their families left behind?" Grain enquired.

A wicked gleam appearing in the dragon's eye, he licked his lips and laughed. "Of course I care about any of their kin. That's why I always eat them as well. We can't have any young ones starving slowly to death can we?"

"Have you no pity?" Grain shouted as he suddenly felt an intense loathing for the giant predator.

"None" Snarfle stated coldly, "now back to business. If you free me as you say you can. I will give you some dragon fire and let you go upon your way without being frazzled."

Grain stood, with his arms hanging loosely by his side as he weighed up the deal that had been offered to him. But he was troubled, because although he knew that time was running out for Toby; he didn't want the responsibility of releasing a creature like Snarfle back upon this, or any other world. Taking another glance over at the bottle, which was still floating in mid-air he said sadly. "Because of the burning desire that you have to eat everything and everyone, I have to reluctantly withdraw my offer."

"What!" Snarfle yelled angrily as he sucked in his breath. "I'll blast you from here to eternity."

Changing into a Saturnian speed ball Grain started bouncing up and down just as the irate dragon sent a fiery burst of flames in his direction.

Using his lightning reflexes, the sandman managed to avoid the lethal blast as another flash of gold and orange flames shot over his head. Moving fast, he managed to stay out of line of fire. “Now Flint” he yelled as he bounced left, then right.

Stunned into action by the sandman’s call, Flint ran and dived through the air, just as old Snarfle was sucking in his breath for another sustained burst. “Got it” Flint yelled in triumph as he trapped a small trace of golden flame in the glass container. Inserting its stopper in mid-air, he landed and rolled clear, all in one movement. “Now let’s get out of here old timer” he shouted, as he slipped behind the safety of the thick granite.

“Soon as possible” Grain answered, as he continued avoiding the searing bolts of death and destruction.

“I’ll catch you eventually” Snarfle bellowed as his rage intensified.

Seizing the window of opportunity that the dragon’s words had created, Grain replied cheekily “not this time” as he ricocheted off the far wall to freedom. Safe behind the cover of the rock face he changed back into monkey form and cried “what happens now shadow-man?”

Making himself visible Flint cried “we get Toby back to the castle before it’s too late.”

“Why?” Grain asked him, needing to know his reason for helping them.

“Because I promised that I’d repay him” Flint croaked “and I always pay my debts.”

"A shadow-man with honour" Grain retorted, "don't make me laugh."

"Believe what you will" Flint shouted. "But at moment I think that you should put aside your petty grievances and concentrate on getting your young companion back to Seaple's or he will surely die."

"Very well" the sandman answered sternly. "But mark my words, if you try and harm him, you will have me to answer to."

Handing over the glass phial that held the fourth element. Flint only grinned as he faded into thin air.

"Drat it" Grain remarked to himself as he sprinted back toward the cave's entrance. "Now I'm beholding to a remorseless killer..."

Reaching the others with the dragon's blood curdling roars still ringing in his ears Grain looked back over his shoulder to see if the shadow man was still there. Seeing no sign of him, he turned his attention to Toby. "How is he?" he asked, looking concerned.

"He's worse" Beearney said, as he fanned him gently with his wing. "Did you get it?" he asked.

"Yeah, I, we got it" Grain responded.

"We?" Beearney asked instantly.

"Yes, we," the sandster confessed. "Flint helped."

"But he works for the stinger Queen?" Beearney cried as he started looking around nervously.

Grain put his hand upon his thick neck and whispered, "maybe he does and maybe he doesn't.

Only time will really tell, but he sure helped me out in there. If it wasn't for him I'd probably just be a smouldering pile of ash by now. Although he may turn out to be a bad un in the end, let's give him the benefit of the doubt for now. At least until he proves us wrong."

"Well said" Flint chipped in, making himself visible again.

"It's you" Grain responded, "I thought you had gone."

"Hoped I'd gone more like" Flint corrected.

The sandman nodded, "true, but as you are still here are you going to help us?" He stared skyward at the thousands of black dots still circling high over head. "Or are you in league with that pack of jackals?"

Walking over to Toby, Flint picked him up in his muscular arms.

"What are you doing?" Grain demanded as he formed his arms into two sharp swords.

"Calm down" Flint said firmly, as he came across as someone that was neither frightened or alarmed easily. "Look I said that I'd help the youngster if I could, and I will if you let me."

"What do you suggest?" Grain asked, as he remained alert and ready to defend his friend.

Flint smiled showing three rows of perfect formed white teeth. "This" he said as he swirled his long cloak in the air, making them both disappear.

"Where are they?" Roland cried in alarm.

"We're still here" Flint rasped, "I'm just demonstrating the wonderful ability of my cloak."

"We can't all fit under there" Grain protested.

Flint became visible again and clasped Toby protectively into his chest. "I've seen these symptoms many times before as I have sneaked around the zone. Death will take him soon unless he has the antidote to the drugs that he's been given. So what are you going to do, let him die or give him the chance to live?"

Grain pondered upon the question, knowing that it would cost Toby his life if he got it wrong. Realising that any chance was better than none he answered "what do you suggest?"

"Good" Flint said as he grabbed a hold of his cloak once more. "You three distract those mangy critters above for as long as you can while I hot foot it back to the castle with him under my cloak."

"Agreed" Grain replied, as Toby and the shadow-man faded into the light of day.

"Are we doing the right thing?" Beearney asked.

"Who knows?" Grain answered despondently. "But the decision has been made, right or wrong. So let's just do our part and pray that Flint does his."

"What's your plan?" the buzzer asked.

"Plan, hmm plan. Yes, well for once I think I have actually got one." He laughed as he beckoned them closer saying. "We are going to take them upon a wild goose chase that they will never forget." Turning to Roland he asked "how are you feeling?"

“I’m fine now that we are out of that heat” he responded.

“Good” Grain relied with a sly grin upon his face “that jungle juice must be darn good stuff. So hang on tight because if you fall off we won’t be coming back for you.”

Climbing onto the buzzer’s back Roland tucked his knees into his thick coarse hair and taking hold of his mane he shouted “now let’s go get em!”

Leaving the cave entrance Grain cried “right now let’s head for the nearest doorway that opens into beach world.

“Why beach world?” Beearney questioned..

“You’ll see when we get there” Grain replied as they gained a lot of height to ensure that they were easily spotted. Quickly accelerating to full speed, they shot away. As the ranting stinger Queen and her army of buzzing drones dived to try and cut them off. But with Beearney flying as fast as he could and a rejuvenated Grain keeping up easily, the trio soon put some distance between themselves and their angry pursuers. “Now we slow down a bit” the sandman shouted. “We don’t want to lose them.”

Easing back upon his wing beats Beearney let the Grainster draw alongside him. “Just over the other side of this ridge is a river” he said. “If we follow it for several miles there’s a portal that goes into sludge world, then another that joins beach world.”

“It’s lucky for us that you know so much about the hidden doorways” Grain remarked.

Beearney chuckled, "my mis-spent youth."

As they reached the door that separated the two worlds the eagle eyed buzzer found the opening mechanism instantly with his keen eyesight. Opening it quickly, they shot through into a very dreary sludge world which was a bubbling mixture of brown and grey goo and gunk. Turning around Beearney expected the sandy coloured buzzer to follow them in but was surprised to see that Grain was sat in the doorway, keeping it open. "They're getting awfully close" Beearney cried as the whole stinger nation bore down on them.

Waiting as long as he could, the sandster slipped out of the entrance at the last moment just as the first snarling stingers grabbed and secured the doorway. "See you soon" he shouted as he hurried off to join his anxious companions.

"Having fun?" Beearney asked, as he questioned Grain's sanity.

"Not really" his stony faced his friend retorted. "But we gotta make sure that they don't get lost." Moving off again at speed, Beearney took the lead once more as they headed toward the next portal that led into beach world. A pale faced Roland just kept his eyes shut and held on tight. Swivelling his neck around, Grain looked back to see several stingers holding the doorway open while the enraged queen and her minions poured through. Shocked by the speed that they were closing, the sandman overtook Beearney and beckoned him to go faster.

"I wish you'd make your mind up" the buzz bomb cried, as he drew alongside.

"How soon will we reach my world? Grain asked, ignoring his comment."

"About two hours" Beearney called back. "I wonder how the others are doing?"

"I don't know" Grain responded "but I hope they are okay."

"Me too" the buzzer yelled. "Now let's lead these horrible little stinkers into whatever it is that you're planning for them."

Flint ran as fast as he could back toward the portal knowing that Drucilla was ready and waiting to open the door when needed. As he watched the entire stinger nation disappear after the others. He knew that it would be plain sailing to get Toby back to the castle, as long as he didn't die along the way. Increasing his pace he ran again, until his lungs were nearly bursting. "At last" he yelled as he finally reached the hidden doorway. Dropping to one knee, he studied Toby momentarily as he hovered between life and death. "Hang on" he begged him, "just a little longer." Grabbing Toby's armlet he pressed the button, and the entrance to Seaple's world opened. He jumped through, but found that they were still some way off from the castle. Taking a deep breath he ran again until he reached the castle steps. Bounding up them two at the time he barged open the doors and cried aloud. "Drucilla, bring the antidote, Toby's dying."

Drucilla appeared almost instantly carrying the large needle that she had frightened her reluctant patient with several days earlier. Sliding down the banister gracefully, she landed at the bottom of the stairs and ran over. “What have you done to him?” she demanded as she gave him a large dose of medicine from the hypodermic needle.

“Saved his life hopefully” Flint answered as he suddenly realised that his face was still exposed.

“Are you on our side now or do I need to call security?” She asked as she gave Toby another shot.

“No need for them” Flint responded.

“Good” she answered, as she glared at him with distrust in her eyes. “Bring him upstairs to the cold room. It will help stabilise him while the antidote helps his nervous system re-acclimatise to this atmosphere.”

With the muscles in his arms aching from having carried Toby so far. Flint winced with pain as he picked him up and followed Drucilla up the staircase to the cold room. “Will he be all right?” he asked as he laid him down gently upon a chilled bed, next to the ashen faced body of Seaple.

“We can only wait and see” Drucilla confessed. “Where are the others and did they manage to collect the four elements? Because the gravity machine is nearing the point of total collapse.”

“They’ve got them” Flint whispered hoarsely. “But I don’t know where they are now?”

“Keep this door open until the last minute” Grain ordered Beearney and Roland. As he glided down to beach world.

“They’re coming!” Roland warned as he watched the yellow and black mass approaching quickly.

“We can’t go yet” the worried buzzer answered. “We have got to make sure that the door doesn’t close completely on them.

“Let’s go now?” Roland demanded impatiently.

“No! Beearney yelled, “not yet.”

“Please!” Roland screamed in despair as thousands of angry stingers thrust their poisonous stings forward into attack position.

“Now!” The buzzer shouted as they left the doorway and scooted away. Stopping abruptly, he spun around to make sure that the armoured insects had managed to secure it and wedge it open. “They’ve made it” he said, suddenly realising that they were only just behind them. “Blimey!” he yelled in alarm, as they shot away at speed.

“Watch out!” Roland screamed as a stinger suddenly lunged at them from the side.

Where did he come from? Beearney wondered, as he changed course quickly and saw the dangerous foe shoot by. “That was to close for comfort” he shouted to his frightened passenger as a powerful jet of water just missed them, hitting a second stinger full in the face. ‘Knocked unconscious, he spiralled out of control, straight into the blood red ocean. Seeing another of their enemies taken out by a second bone shattering strike, Beearney stole a quick peek below, to see an army of sea scooters in battle formation. “Wow!” He trilled “now that’s what I call a navy.” The sky suddenly full of salvos of salt water. He nimbly picked his way through them until a large ball of compacted sand nearly took his head off. “Crikey what was that!” he shrieked as he veered violently to his left to avoid it. Still cursing, he stared down to see Grain orchestrating ten thousand sandy coloured arms which were all happily tossing sand missiles with gay abandon. “Lunatic!” he yelled as the maniacal sandman caught his eye and waved furiously.

Although the stingers were battered by the constant barrage of powerful water jets and sand missiles for several miles. As Grain rejoined his waiting companions, his face was still showing concern. “We must have brought down hundreds” he cried, “but they still keep coming.”

“What now?” Beearney asked as he narrowly avoided yet another lump of wet sand.

“Same as before” Grain replied, as a sly smile appeared upon his face. “But this time we lead them to the old whistle snorer.”

Pinning back their ears, they sprinted for the next portal. As they opened it Grain shouted “you two get going, I’ll catch you up later. There’s something that I have to do first.”

“Can’t we help?” Roland asked, opening his eyes for the first time in a long while.

“No!” Grain barked in answer “you can’t. The only way that you can only help me now is if you do what I ask. So get going and get the others to fortify the castle's defences. If I can't stop the stingers here with my next strategy, it will be down to you. Now go while you still can."

Beearney took a final glance at the oncoming swarm of stingers and reluctantly did what he was told knowing that the Sandman's chances of survival were slim.

Grain watched his comrades fade into the distance, and leaving it until the very last moment; he slipped away from the door. As the stinger vanguard secured it and started prising open the last barrier between them and their long awaited prize, the gravity machine. Trying something that he'd never tried before Grain split into two pieces and formed himself into a copy of Beearney and Roland and a second buzzer. Hoping that he could fool the enemy for a short time, reaching the whistle snorer in next to no time, he was pleasantly surprised to see that his pursuers were still giving chase. Circling the giant contorted tree he awaited for the deadly swarm's imminent arrival.

Finding himself completely surrounded by a sky full of angry stinger warriors, he waited patiently, while the stinger Queen flew forward to gloat over her trapped quarry. "So we meet again sandbag," She said. "But I assure you that I won't underestimate you this time."

"We shall see" Grain responded dryly as he merged both his halves into a large propeller.

Watching him spinning furiously the Queen laughed "he's gone mad, kill the old fool!" As several drone warriors moved into finish off their adversary, the old whistle snorer started singing its lullaby, in a high pitched whistle. “Sleep, sleep, go to sleep.”

“What’s happening?” the baffled Queen demanded as her drones started falling asleep and fell from the sky.

“Sleep, sleep” the whistle snorer sang as he continued singing his song of slumber.

“Wake up or I will suck you all dry!” bellowed the angry monarch as tried to scare her troops into staying awake. But her eyes becoming weary, all thoughts of conquest were overtaken by the sudden desire to sleep as she too succumbed to the old tree’s magical spell.

“Yippee!” Grain cried as he cheered his victory. Then he wondered just how long he could keep spinning, for he was getting tired already after having been chased all over the zone. I know that I can’t keep this up indefinitely he thought, but at least I can give everyone else some breathing space.

As daylight slowly faded giving way to night, he began slowing down as he fought his body’s irrepressible demand to rest. Falling wearily to the floor in a state of distress he cried “water, need water.” He started crawling back toward the doorway that led to beach world but before he had gone very far, stingers started to awaken around him. With great determination he reformed his aching body into a propeller again and tried to rise and start spinning once more. But collapsed as the Queen's horny hoof pushed him back down and injected him with a lethal dose of poison.

Chapter Eight
The Fifth Element

Landing at the castle Beearney and Roland made their way up to the door, but found it barred. After a lot of knocking, kicking and hammering, a security guard finally let them in. "About time" Beearney remarked angrily as they flew up the stairs. "Did they make it, where's Flint and Toby?"

"They made it all right" Drucilla answered, as she appeared from nowhere and leaned upon the balustrade. "Follow me" she said as she walked away with her long green hair flowing gracefully behind her.

"How is he?" Roland shouted anxiously as they caught her up, and followed her down the long corridor.

"See for yourself" she answered as she flung a large wooden door open.

"Toby!" they both cried together "you're all right."

“Never felt better” he responded as a broad smile lit up his face.

“Thank our lucky stars” Beearney said as he ran over and sat next to him.

“Flint’s the one to thank” Toby corrected. “Without his help I wouldn’t have made it.”

“Good for him” the buzzer shouted. Unable to contain himself he did a little buzzer dance but stopped, as he noticed that the shadow-man who was sat in the corner. Hovering over to him immediately, he bowed in gratitude. “Well done” he said gratefully.

“The pleasure was all mine” Flint replied as he took a deep drag upon a long wooden pipe. Leaning forward in his chair the rugged looking shadow-man added. “Perhaps it’s I that should thank you because it’s been a long time since I could hold my head up high.”

Sitting back upon the edge of the bed beside Toby. Beearney asked him “how he was feeling?”

“Not too bad” Toby replied “where’s Grain?”

Unable to look Toby in the eye, Beearney stared at the wall. “He stayed behind” he said.

“But he promised not to take any more risks” Toby shouted. “Now tell me why and don’t leave anything out.”

“I’ll gladly tell you all about what happened to us later if we get the opportunity. All you really need to know for now is that Grain sacrificed himself to buy us some time.”

Tears running down his face, Toby cried “ time, time for what?”

“To prepare for a stinger attack, because they’re on the way.”

“I don’t wish to interrupt your little reunion” Ducilla said abruptly. “But which one of you has the stuff?”

“Grain,” Roland whispered quietly. The realisation hitting home that the stinger Queen now had in her possession the four elements.

“Great” Drucilla shouted angrily “what do we do now?”

Sitting up in his bed Toby wiped his cheeks and declared solemnly. “We prepare to welcome for our royal guest.”

“You gotta be joking?” Drucilla responded “she’ll kill us all.”

“Very likely” Toby agreed. “But we can’t do anything without the four elements can we. So we need to meet her face to face, and if we play our cards right we may just get lucky.”

“Have you got a plan though?” Flint enquired blowing a smoke ring high into the air.

“Not really” Toby answered as he swung his legs over the bed and started putting on his shoes. “We are going to have to improvise.”

As Beearney left the castle to greet the invading army, two things happened that shook him badly. The first was when the stinger warrior’s opened up before him like the red sea to let him pass. The second was that as he approached the dreaded stinger Queen, he saw Grain, who was covered from head to foot in a hard honey casing.

Seeing the shock upon the buzzer's face the Monarch laughed as she rolled the trapped Sandman beneath her bony hooves. "I see that you have noticed that I have captured my Father's murderer. He's not quite dead yet, but it shouldn't be too much longer by the look of him. But that's stinger venom for you, kills most things in the end."

Trying to ignore the taunt and the terrible position that he saw his good friend in, Beearney bowed as befitted a visiting member of royalty. "Welcome your majesty" he stated loudly. "If you will follow me I will take you to talk with the custodian, who is expecting you."

"Why should I talk?" she demanded pompously. "When my drones can just walk in and take over?"

"Because it may be in your interest" the buzzer replied, as he tried to disguise his loathing of her. He watched her as she sat considering his offer while reclining in her black onyx chair, which was being carried six of her foot soldiers.

She grinned replying sarcastically "very well, just because I am in a good mood." Snarling, she stamped upon her prisoner underfoot. "Not that it will do any of you any good. But just remember horse face, if you or any of the others try anything funny I will finish off this miserable old sandman." Digging in her hooves hard again, to emphasise her point, Beearney winced as he heard Grain groan with pain.

Managing to keep his calm, he bowed. Stating ceremoniously "this way your majesty please."

"I want every exit secured by the time I come back out or else!" she bellowed as she and her personal escort followed the buzzer into the castle through the maze of winding corridors that led down to the secret room below.

Beearney felt her hot breath upon his back as she got closer, and sensing his unease, she whispered coldly "and when this is over I will invade your home land and kill everyone there."

He felt the short stubby hairs on his neck rise, but said nothing in response as he guided his unwelcome visitor into the secret room where Toby, Drucilla, Seaple and Roland were all waiting. "Well, well look what we have here. A welcome party consisting of an old raga muffin and some silly children. Now this is a sight to put fear into the new ruler of the zone."

"Darvock thought the same" Seaple croaked weakly, propping himself up on his elbow.

"I'm not my father" the queen shrieked as she angrily rolled the honey coated Grain into the gravity machine. Smashing into a thousand pieces, the casing spewed his orange coloured body onto the tiled floor. "Because I always win" she added.

Looking down at Grain's battered body Toby noticed that the small leather pouch containing the four elements was still around his neck. Moving over to him slowly he said "oh great and powerful Queen, I salute you and your famous victory. But I would add one word of caution on this, your day of destiny. For the opportunity for greatness can be fleeting. So, as all great leaders must, you must also grasp an opportunity when it presents itself."

"Meaning?" she asked, as she watched Toby gently take the small bag off the fading sandman.

"Meaning this" he declared as he held the hard earned fruits of their quest on high. When you sent the shadow-man Flint to sabotage the gravity machine, you made a grave error. For it is not just damaged as you intended. It is on the point of total collapse, and you must realise where that leaves you. For when it blows, and you mark my words it will blow soon, everything in the Solar System will be destroyed. On my world we call it Armageddon; here you probably call it something different. But it all comes down to the same thing in the end. Your dreams of total colonisation will be over." He stood upon the step of the gravity machine. "This is the wondrous piece of technology" he said. "You had it, but you blew it, literally."

Rushing towards him the irate Queen shrieked "I'll tear your head off."

Holding his ground Toby shouted back "and kill the only person that can repair it!"

Stopping just before she reached him, she clenched her cloven hooves in anger as his mind numbing words slowly registered in her brain. Retreating somewhat she softened her tone, asking "only you?"

"Yes, only me" he stated adamantly as he checked inside the pouch to see if the four containers were still there. Seeing that they were, he moved onto the next part of his hastily concocted plan to get her to let him try and repair it.

"Do you intend to repair it?" She enquired casually.

"Maybe" he responded, "but what's the point if you are going to kill us any way?"

"I may let you live" she lied.

"I doubt it" Toby said.

"What if we cut a deal" she asked, "what would it take?"

Toby sat down upon the step as he pondered upon what concessions would help their situation the most. "Can you help him?" he asked, pointing to the grainster.

"Possibly" she conceded, "but it's asking far too much. He's the one that killed my Father."

"Right" Toby agreed sarcastically as he tried to think of something else that they needed. But his mind suddenly becoming blank through fear, he just couldn't think of any thing else that could help them. Playing for time as much as anything else he said softly "if you help him and spare our lives, including all the castle staff, I will repair the gravity machine."

"You strike a hard bargain" she said as she held out her hairy limb to shake on it.

Taking the enormous hoof in his tiny hand Toby could see the hidden malice in her eyes. But trying not to show the gut wrenching fear that he felt in the pit of his stomach he said "deal. But as a sign of good faith you must help Grain first."

"If I must" she said, walking over to the crumpled sandman she injected a red liquid into his head.

The dark orange colour draining from his face, Toby watched as his normal sandy colour came back, and he knew that the stinger Queen had done as asked.

"There" she whispered "I've helped him as I said I would. Now you must fulfil your side of the bargain."

"Fine" Toby declared "and I will. But just give me a few minutes with my colleagues first.

"Very well" she agreed "but not too long."

"A moment" Toby assured her, as he made his way over to where Seaple, Drucilla and Roland were watching his performance in disbelief. Flint was also near, but he was cloaked.

"Are you mad?" Drucilla whispered. "We can't let her get her grubby mitts on the gravity machine."

"I know that" Toby said "trust me, although I don't really know what's going to happen next. I feel that what I am doing is right."

"I hope that it is" Drucilla responded quietly.

"Just go for it" Roland added.

"Yes my young friend, do what you think is right and follow your conscience." Seaple suggested in barely more than a whisper.

"Are you there Mr Flint?" Toby said quietly.

"I'm here Toby and watching her every movement. I'll do whatever I can to help, so be lucky."

"I'll try" he answered as the stinger Queen demanded belligerently "are you going to be all day?"

"Coming" he replied as he turned to face the giant piece of machinery. But as he stood there, bag in hand he realised that the real test was ahead. For he didn't have a clue where to start. Deciding to try to solve the puzzle in a logical fashion, he studied the four small bottles carefully. He tried to fathom the sequence that they needed to be fitted in, earth, wind, fire and water he thought, what can the pattern be? Then it seemed obvious to him, as if someone or something had suddenly planted the answer in his head. "First came the earth as a growing medium" he proclaimed as he opened the tiny bottle and placed its contents in the niche on his far left. "Then came water to enable life to develop in the earth" he added, pouring the tiny drop of life giving liquid into the niche on his far right. "Third came wind to agitate the oceans and stimulate the atmosphere." He said as he placed the tiny wisp of swirling blue light into position. Taking the fourth phial he opened it and placed its contents upon the palm of his hand. "Fire" he declared" that which burns within worlds, helping life develop with its warmth." He stood back as the huge machine started humming and started operating normally. Until it stopped as quickly as it started and became silent again.

"Fraud!" the angry Queen screamed, "no one cheats me and lives."

"Wait" Toby cried "it's only a glitch, I'll fix it."

“I’ll fix you more like” she screeched, as she bore down upon him.

Toby automatically put out his hands to protect himself from the irate stinger Queen.

Realising the danger that Toby was in Flint rugby tackled her, sending her flying to where a partially recovered Grain hit her with a karate chop. Pushing him aside the she yelled “It’s Flint, get him.” But before any of her had drones could react, the shadow-man had rolled clear and wrapped himself in his cloak again. Enraged by his disappearance she renewed her attack on Toby again but stopped in her tracks as two long probes from the gravity machine slipped into his ears. “What more trickery?” she cried as she sprang at him with her tail coiled to strike. Flying backwards immediately with great force, she struck the wall hard and fell to the floor. Getting up she flew at him again, with the same consequence.

“What’s happening?” Drucilla asked Seaple curiously.

With a wry smile the old custodian whispered. “The new custodian is defending the zone and all its inhabitants.”

“But I thought that I was going to be the new custodian?” Drucilla moaned.

“So did I” Seaple declared, “but it seems that the gravity machine has other ideas.”

Pulling herself up unceremoniously from the floor for the second time, the injured Queen beckoned her drones to attack her enemy. Moving forward as one, they converged upon their quarry but found that he was too strong. As he effortlessly threw them through the air, landing awkwardly in a heap, some lay still while others tried to stand and attack once more. Propelled through the air again, they lay scattered upon the ground like nine pins. Realising that brute force wasn't working the Queen decided to try the subtle approach. "Bravo!" she cried "very impressive indeed. As I imagined you would be." Moving closer she bowed low, as she awaited the chance to strike!

Toby watched her as she came nearer "that's close enough" he said cautiously.

Ignoring his request the battered monarch crept closer. "But my lord" she cried "you have won the respect and allegiance of the stinger Nation." Eyeing him with evil intent she edged just a little nearer.

"Stay back!" Toby ordered her "or I will be forced to defend myself."

Taking another two more small steps, she got ready to whip her lethal tail over her head.

"Watch her" she's still dangerous Seaple warned.

"I know" Toby responded gratefully. "But every creature should have the opportunity to change their ways and leave in peace. Because the age of magic and war is over, making way for the age of peace and reason" He stared directly into the Queen's eyes, hoping to see some sign of capitulation but he only saw a desire to rule and cause pain. "I ask you again" he begged "give up this senseless folly and return to your own world in peace."

"Never!" She screamed as she brought down her stinger with all her might.

Deflecting her blow with the powerful forces that flowed through him. Toby watched in horror as the stinger Queen's momentum took her lethal sting into the gravity machine. As electricity poured into her shaking body, the two silver probes retracted out of his ears. He watched her as she writhed and shrieked in agony.

As her burning body finally stopped moving, he turned to the others and declared "it's over."

"Quite" Seaple agreed, as he touched his forehead in acknowledgement of his successor.

"Hoorah!" Beearney and Roland shouted as they echoed Seaple's sentiments.

"Hail the new custodian" Flint cried as he sank to one knee in homage.

"Show off" Drucilla whined as they all cheered him and praised their victory. But overcoming her disappointment quickly, she too cheered as loud as everyone else.

As the two morning suns filtered through the castle window, Toby and the others were summoned to a meeting called by Seaple. As they sat around the long wooden table he made a short statement. "Although a new custodian has been chosen by the gravity machine, I have decided to stay on as caretaker until he is ready to take over. Although I accept that Toby has proven himself beyond question, I feel at thirteen he just isn't ready to manage his new appointment." He smiled as he stared at the scrawny little Earth child that he had doubted. "So I will stay on until his sixteenth birthday. If that's acceptable of course? he added.

"It is" Toby said, as he suddenly realised that it was his fourteenth birthday today.

Seeing the look of shock upon his face, the custodian clapped his hands and his cook brought in a large cake. "Come on" he said "blow the candles out."

Hesitating momentarily, Toby thought how he usually got up early on his birthday so that he could spend some time with his Mum and Dad before going to school. But not wanting to spoil the party he extinguished them all, although his heart wasn't really in it.

"Well done" they all cried, as they sang a rousing chorus of Happy Birthday. Calling them quickly back to order, Seaple became serious once again. "Okay that's enough of the mushy stuff because there are one or two more things to discuss. First the stinger army has vowed to return to their home world and never go to war again. This leaves us with one final task, to say our farewells to Toby and Roland until we meet them again in the future." Getting up one by one the assembled group came around the table to say their goodbyes. First came Flint the Shadow-man "until we meet again" he said.

"You bet" Toby whispered.

Next it was Beearney, who glided around the table and hovered as he rubbed his head into Toby's cheek. "I'll really miss you" he cried, tears forming in his eyes.

"I'll miss you too" Toby agreed.

Strutting her stuff confidently. Drucilla leaned upon the corner of the table, flashing her green eyes seductively. "Well half pint," she teased. "Are you going to miss me?"

"Like mad" Toby replied honestly.

"Good" she responded, "remember I'll be missing you too."

"You will?" He asked dumbly.

"Not!" She cried, as she walked away laughing.

"She will really" Seaple said as he took his turn. "Don't worry about her or anything else. Just enjoy the next couple of years; we will both be here when you return."

"I'll try to, but it will be hard, being apart from you all" Toby answered.

Last but not least came Grain, who had almost completely recovered.

"Hi there" he said "how does it feel being the new custodian?"

"Not very different" Toby confessed. "I certainly don't feel like the great warrior or wizard.

Grain smiled, as only he could, from ear to ear. "Greatness comes in many forms" he said. "Strength, wisdom or other ways. Like the ability to motivate others into doing deeds that they wouldn't normally do. You may not realise it youngster, but you are infectious with your honesty and willingness to help."

"Like a disease" Drucilla teased.

"I will miss you" Grain continued.

"As I will you" Toby replied.

"Oh Toby" Seaple interrupted, "there's some people outside that I'd like you meet"

"Who?" Toby enquired.

"Your Mum and Dad of course" he responded.

"Mum, Dad!" he yelled as he saw them entering the room. "How's it possible?"

"Anything's possible now the gravity machine is operating properly again" Seaple assured him.

Running over to them, his Mother swept him up in her arms and showered him with kisses while his Dad ruffled his hair, enjoying the moment.

Roland turned away disappointed, with tears welling up in his eyes. Suddenly, he heard his Father call out softly "hello son." Spinning around quickly he ran over and hugged him.

Printed in the United States
65871LVS00001B/94

9 781425 954871